GR

Raven Hill Mysteries

GREEN FOR DANGER

Raven Hill Mysteries 6

Emily Rodda
&
John St Claire

Hodder
Children's
Books

a division of Hodder Headline plc

Series concept copyright © Emily Rodda 1994
Text copyright © Ashton Scholastic 1994

First published in Australia in 1994 by
Ashton Scholastic Pty Limited

First published in Great Britain in 1996
by Hodder Children's Books

10 9 8 7 6 5 4 3 2 1

A Catalogue record for this book is available from
the British Library

ISBN 0 340 62996 7

Typeset by Avon Dataset Ltd, Bidford-on-Avon
Printed and bound in Great Britain by
Cox & Wyman Ltd, Reading, Berkshire

Hodder Children's Books
a division of Hodder Headline plc
338 Euston Road
London NW1 3BH

Contents

1

The rip-off

It's Friday the thirteenth, and the six of us are standing at the front door of the mansion known all over Raven Hill as 'Terzis Castle'.

We're right on time, neat and tidy and responsible-looking, and on the trail of a nice, quiet, comfortable house-sitting job for some old friends of my family. No problems, for once, I'd told the others. No problems. Right?

Wrong.

I raise my hand to ring the bell, Liz, Sunny, Elmo, Tom and Richelle paste pretty smiles on their faces, and what happens? The door flies open, nearly knocking me flat, and this huge guy with a stocking over his face and blood streaming from his forehead comes staggering out, waving a knife.

We forget our manners and don't wait to say hello. We dive for cover. And he doesn't wait either. He weaves down the path with both hands stretched out in front of him as if he's blind. Then a car reverses up to the gate like it's being driven by a madman, the passenger door jerks open and the guy falls in. The car screams off.

And suddenly it's very quiet. The smoke from the car's exhaust drifts in the street. The smell of burning rubber from its tyres hangs in the air. Blood dries on the path. We look at each other. I wonder if I'm as pale as everyone else. I breathe out, for the first time in minutes.

Richelle crawls to her feet and glares at me. 'I thought you said this job would be easy, Nick Kontellis,' she says. She points at her grubby knees. 'Do you realise these jeans were clean on this morning?'

○

Afterwards, when we were talking to the cops, I felt a bit weak. Especially when I found out what the guy had done. But what were we supposed to do? Trip him up and sit on him? I don't think so.

Sure, there were six of us, but this guy was big—I mean *really* big. Like if this guy had had wheels, he would have been a truck. Besides, there was the knife. A small point, but worth considering.

All the same, it was a drag having to say we hadn't seen the driver of the car. If we'd been able to give a description, that would have been something. As it was, all we could say for sure was that it was a man. Well, that eliminated half the population.

That must have been a big help.

●

Here's what had happened:

Mr Terzis had arrived home from his jewellery shop at the usual time. Mrs Terzis was out playing cards, like she always did on Friday afternoons.

Mr T hadn't seen anything suspicious at first. He was just coming home after work. Just like he did after any other long day of selling diamond necklaces to people who had more money than they knew what to do with, and wedding rings to people who think they're going to be married forever and friendship rings to people nobody would want to know.

Anyway, he put his key in the front door lock and then suddenly felt the cold steel of a knife blade on the side of his neck.

'One sound and you're dead meat, old man!' a voice said. 'Open that door and make it quick!'

Mr Terzis did as he was told. A man pushed him through the doorway. Claws clattered on the floor as Pedro and Pepita, the two little chihuahuas rushed, yapping, out to greet him.

'Unlock the deadlock on the inside,' the man ordered. 'Turn off the alarm. You've got thirty seconds. And if that red light comes on, you're history!'

(Point number one: the intruder knew about the alarm. A lucky guess?)

Mr Terzis punched the numbers into the keypad,

glancing sideways at the man as he did. He didn't have a hope of recognising the guy because of the stocking pulled over his face. The little dogs were jumping around his ankles, barking their heads off. He murmured to them softly, to quieten them. He didn't want the man to get angry and hurt them.

Mr T could have pushed the alarm button and the bell would have gone off down in the cop shop. There wasn't a siren in the house but the red light would have flashed on the keypad, the guy would have seen it, and Mr T would have been shark bait. He knew his wife wouldn't like that. And he wasn't too keen about the idea, either.

When the light flashed green, Mr Terzis breathed a sigh of relief.

'Now. Upstairs. To the safe!' the man yelled.

(Point number two: he *knew* there was a safe upstairs. Two lucky guesses in a row, maybe. Or—)

Mr Terzis felt his stomach turn over. Oh, no, not again, he thought.

'There's nothing in the safe you'd want,' he protested aloud. 'Just papers.'

'Do as I say!' The knife pressed a little harder against his neck.

Mr Terzis began walking through his big, beautiful living room, towards the waterfall fountain, the glass-walled orchid house, the stairs. Pedro and Pepita rushed ahead of him, skittering on the floor. The roses he'd bought for his wife yesterday bloomed red as blood on the white marble coffee table. His good leather shoes tapped on the shiny white marble floor. Sweat ran down his neck into the collar of his expensive shirt. His knees felt like jelly.

He tried again at the foot of the stairs. On one side of him, the waterfall splashed softly. On the other side, the orchids bloomed. 'You're making a big mistake. There's nothing in the safe. Everything of value is in the city—in the shop,' he said.

'Don't lie, old man. Upstairs! Come on, and make it snappy!'

(Point number three: the guy in the mask knew there was something in the safe. He *knew* it. You could hear it in his voice. No lucky guess this time.)

Mr Terzis thought about that for a minute. Thought about the other two lucky guesses, too. He wondered about them. And then, because he hadn't come to Australia and built up a million-dollar business from nothing without being a pretty cool sort of character, he put them out of his mind.

There were more important things to think about just now. Like the knife at his neck. And whether this thug was as tough as he sounded. And, most of all, what would happen if he lost what was in that safe.

He started climbing to the first floor. Pedro and Pepita sat down at the foot of the stairs, whined, and cocked their ears. They weren't allowed upstairs. And they couldn't understand why their master was going there instead of out into the kitchen as he usually did when he got home.

Even on a good day, Mr Terzis wasn't one for leaping up his stairs two at a time, but tonight he was trying for the

Guinness Book of Records slow-stair-climbing championship.

Halfway up, he stopped. 'What are you going to do?' he asked, playing for time.

'*I'm* not going to do anything,' the man snarled. '*You're* going to open the safe. The safe in your workroom.'

(Point number four: he even knew where the safe *was*!)

'I told you, all the gems are at the shop,' Mr Terzis said.

'Get moving!'

There was no way out. Mr Terzis led the man upstairs to his workroom. His eyes slid to the switch on the wall. The other burglar alarm switch. The master. Its light was showing green. But if he could reactivate it—brush against it, maybe, or . . .

'Don't even think about it,' growled the man in the stocking mask, gesturing at the switch. The knife nudged a little harder.

Mr Terzis pulled the bookcase aside and opened the safe in the wall behind it. Inside was a small stack of velvet jewellery boxes.

'Open them!' the man ordered.

One by one, Mr Terzis opened the boxes. Each time the man took a quick look and then whacked the contents onto the floor with his free hand. In seconds, bracelets, rings and necklaces were scattered on the carpet like confetti at a wedding.

'These are rubbish!' the man yelled. 'You know what I'm after! Get them!'

'But this is all I have,' Mr Terzis pleaded.

'The emeralds! Give me the emeralds!'

(Point number five: the guy knew about the emeralds. He knew that Mr Terzis had brought them home from the shop and put them in his safe.)

At that point Mr Terzis realised that he couldn't stall any more. The man knew everything there was to know. Besides, his voice was getting high-pitched and nervy. And if a thug with a knife is dangerous, a nervy thug with a knife is downright deadly.

Mr Terzis reached into the back of the safe and pulled out a small plastic bag. Inside were five ordinary-looking, rough, brown stones with greenish tinges.

He felt as though he was choking on his heart, which seemed to have moved from his chest to his throat. He knew he was holding his life in his hand. Cut and polished, these little stones would be green fire. Worth a fortune. A sheik's ransom. His hand trembled slightly.

The man snatched at the bag with his free hand, and held it up to the light.

'Is this all of them?' he asked finally. 'You'd better not hold out on me, Terzis, or you'll regret it.'

(Point number six: the guy didn't know exactly how many emeralds there were.)

Mr Terzis thought about that. He hesitated a moment too long. The knife pushed hard against his neck again. 'There's more, right?' snarled the man. 'Get them! Quick!'

Mr Terzis let his shoulders slump. Anyone looking at him would have thought he'd given up.

'I'll do it, I'll do it,' he mumbled. 'Just don't hurt me. Please.'

The thug's mouth under the stocking mask twisted into a smile of contempt. He had this rich old pig right where he wanted him. He relaxed.

(Point number seven: first he gets nervy, then he relaxes too soon. And he underestimates his victim. This is starting to look like amateur night.)

He watched as Mr Terzis slowly climbed up on a stool and reached to the top shelf of the bookcase. He was still smiling. Then Mr Terzis turned around, and the smile disappeared.

'Drop the emeralds,' snarled Mr Terzis. The small gun he held in his hand was pointed straight at the man's heart.

2

Deadly game

The man in the stocking mask knew trouble when he saw it. The old guy was angry. The little black gun looked angry too. It was time to leave. He kicked at the stool and made for the door.

As the stool tipped out from under him, Mr Terzis fell heavily to the ground. But he fell firing. A couple of wild bullets ripped into the wall.

'I'll get you for this, you mongrel!' the thug yelled. He darted off to the left. Bad move. The stairs were to the right.

(Point number eight: he wasn't too bright. And he didn't know very much about the upstairs sections of the Terzis house.)

Mr Terzis staggered to his feet, activated the alarm, and pelted after him.

Up here it was like a maze. They ran it. They played a deadly game of tips through plush, empty bedrooms, luxury ensuite bathrooms, sewing room, library, TV room, little corridors.

In a way, they were both running for their lives. The man with the emeralds and the man with the gun. In and out of doors, in and out of rooms, ducking and weaving.

All the man in the stocking mask wanted was to get back to the stairs and get out. All Mr Terzis wanted was a clear shot, his enemy on the floor, and the emeralds back in his hand.

The man with the emeralds was younger and stronger. But Mr Terzis knew the house. That made the chase almost even. But in the end, by sheer luck, the thief burst through a doorway and saw the stairs in front of him.

He leaped for them and began racing down. Pedro and Pepita sprang to their feet and began dancing around, yapping furiously. Mr Terzis ran after the thief, pounding down the stairs and firing again and again. Bullets pecked chips from the steps and sent them flying through the air.

The man in the mask dodged and kept going. He was nearly at the foot of the stairs.

'Stop!' Mr Terzis roared. 'Stop!'

He had only one thing on his mind. To keep the thief, and the emeralds, in the house until the police arrived.

And that was why he jumped, crashing into the thug's back, grabbing him around his neck. They thudded together down the last few stairs. Pedro and Pepita yelped and shot off in opposite directions.

The next thing Mr Terzis knew he was lying half in and half out of the pool at the foot of the stairs. He could hardly breathe. His head was roaring. He must have hit it on the marble edge of the pool, or on one of the rocks.

In the water, under his fingers, he could feel the gun. But he couldn't move, and the man he had wrestled to the ground was staggering to his feet, clambering out of the pool.

Dimly, Mr Terzis could hear him cursing and groaning as he stumbled off, his feet splashing on the marble floor as he broke into a shambling run. He was panicking, making for the family dining room and kitchen. He was going to try to escape through the back door. The little dogs were growling and barking at his heels.

Got you! Mr Terzis mumbled to himself. Because he knew that the back door was deadlocked. There was no way out for the guy in the stocking mask in that direction.

Soon, very soon, the police would be arriving at the front, in response to the alarm. Just a few more minutes, and the emeralds would be safe. A few more . . . He struggled to move, but a wave of pain crashed into his head, turning the world red.

There was a howl of rage from the kitchen, and thudding crashes as the thief hurled himself at the back door. Then feet, accompanied by yapping chihuahua voices, began pelting back over the wet marble towards the front of the house.

Hope you slip and kill yourself, thought Mr Terzis. He was usually a peaceable man, but he'd got pretty fed up with the man in the stocking mask. And, like magic, just at that moment there was a yelp, a slip, a shout, a crash, and a sickening thump.

Mr Terzis lay half in, half out of the pool, helpless as a half-drowned kitten. Stay down, he thought. Stay down.

But this guy was tough. Tough, and desperate. In a few seconds Mr Terzis heard groans and slapping sounds, and the dragging clatter of the knife on the marble floor. He could hear Pedro and Pepita whimpering. Were they hurt?

He couldn't look. He couldn't turn his head. But he knew that the thief was crawling. Crawling, and finally staggering to his feet, and stumbling past him without a look, to the front door.

And that's where we came in. Or rather where we went out— diving for cover while the man in the blood-smeared stocking mask staggered and raved and bled all along the path to the street, and the getaway car roared up and then away.

Elmo and Sunny ran out to the road to wait for the police. We could hear the sirens in the distance, getting louder. A bit late, I thought, and bolted into the house with Liz, Tom and Richelle close behind.

At the arched doorway to the big, open living room I stopped dead. It was some sight. The marble floor was swimming with water. A trail of bloody footprints tracked through the room from the back of the house to the front door. And half in, half out of the fountain pool beside the stairs, with the two little dogs whimpering beside him, sprawled Mr Terzis.

12

I'd been in the Terzis house lots of times. Even when a party was on and people were chatting and laughing around the place, it always looked like something out of one of those glossy magazines. Now it was more like the set of a horror movie. The whiteness, the light, the touches of gold, the softly splashing waterfall, the orchids blooming in the glasshouse, even the red roses on the coffee table, just added to the horrible effect.

Mr Terzis was lying across the waterfall pool wall, with one shoulder in the water. He was absolutely still, and pale, like a wax model. His mouth was hanging open. His nose was running. His grey hair was messy and dripping wet and a huge, ugly-looking lump was swelling on his forehead.

It gave me a bad jolt. It felt like a punch in the stomach. I'd known this guy since I was in nappies. He was a big, powerful, confident, laughing guy, always in control. Like my own father, I guess. Seeing him like this was a shock. Mr Terzis just didn't fit my image of a victim. But here he was—helpless, moaning. I think I thought he was dying.

'Mr Terzis!' I said. Well, I guess I yelled. Like I told you, I'd had a shock. I ran to the pool and knelt down beside him. I didn't know what to do. I was scared to touch him. Pepita nudged me with her small, cold black nose. She was shivering all over.

'Mr Terzis. It's me, Nick,' I said.

He managed to speak. 'Nick. Help. Police,' he mumbled.

'They're coming,' I said.

And they were. You could hear the sirens loudly now.

13

He made himself speak again. I had to lean close so I could hear him. I saw the little black gun lying in the pool, almost covered by weed. It looked like a toy, but I knew it wasn't.

I touched Mr T's hand by accident. It was wet and terribly cold. He turned it with a huge effort and gripped my wrist.

'Emeralds,' he whispered. 'Tell them, Nick. Stop him. He's got . . .'

His eyelids fluttered closed.

I stared at him, feeling the grip of that wet, cold hand. Then Liz was beside me. She was panting. Her hazel eyes looked black.

'I've rung the ambulance, Nick,' she gasped. She stroked the trembling Pedro and Pepita, looked at Mr Terzis's pale face and nibbled at her bottom lip. 'Is he going to be okay?'

I blinked at her. 'I don't know,' I muttered.

Mr Terzis's head rolled from side to side. 'The emeralds,' he muttered. 'Stop him—Nick, please, stop him. Nick, please . . .'

3

The castle

Nick. That's me. Nick Kontellis. I'm not superstitious, but that Black Friday at Terzis Castle really lived up to its name. It was bad for Mr Terzis, bad for Mrs Terzis, bad for me and the rest of the Teen Power gang. And if our luck was bad that day, it got worse from then on. But I'll get to that in a minute.

To go back a bit, we'd come to see about looking after the house while the Terzises went on holiday. That's the sort of thing Teen Power Inc. does.

Teen Power Inc.'s our business. Our motto is 'We'll Do Anything'—and we mean it. Anything legal, anyway. Most of the jobs we get are dead boring. Dog-walking, delivering leaflets, cleaning, helping out in shops—stuff people can get high school kids like us to do for peanut pay without having to feel guilty.

Still, little as it is, the money's a help. Keeps me in computer games, Richelle in clothes and Tom Moysten in hamburgers and Mars bars—just. And we've stumbled into a few nice little mysteries and tricky situations along the way.

More than a few, in fact. That reduces the boredom factor.

We advertise in the local paper, and we get jobs from all over Raven Hill where we live, but the Terzis gig was a personal thing. Teen Power Inc. got it because of me.

Mr and Mrs Terzis are old friends of my parents. They haven't got any kids, and they've always been pretty keen on me—like I'm their favourite nephew, or something.

Mr Terzis and Dad were born in the same village in Greece and came to Australia together when they were young. Dad did okay, but Mr Terzis did better. He's a jeweller and gem-dealer and has mega-rich clients all over the world.

The thing is, Mr T's a real workaholic and Mrs T's been trying to get him to take a holiday for years. He never wants to go anywhere. Too much work to do, he always says. And who'd look after the house? The dogs? The orchids? The fish? The birds? The garden?

But just a few days ago he'd finally caved in.

'Okay, Anna, we go away for one week,' he said, 'but one condition . . .'

The condition was that somebody come in every day to look after the place.

His assistant at the shop, Miles Silvestro, was keen to do it, Mum said. But Mr T wanted him to concentrate on the business. There was more than enough for Miles to cope with there, he said. So then Mrs T thought of me, and Teen Power Inc.

The rest, as they say, is history.

❁

The Terzis house is no ordinary house. It's a huge square white building, with a red tiled roof topped by a big glass dome. From the outside it looks more like a museum than a mansion.

There are no proper windows, only long slits sealed with toughened glass. Too narrow for anyone to get through. Back when I was one of Robin Hood's Merry Men, guys in castles used to shoot arrows out of slits like that to repel invaders.

Anyway, that's why everyone in Raven Hill calls the place 'Terzis Castle'. People who don't know think it must be ultra dark and grim inside. No light, no air.

They couldn't be more wrong.

When you step through the front door it's like walking into another world. The living room, which takes up the whole middle of the house and flows into the dining room and kitchen beyond, is like an open courtyard. The sun shines through a huge glass dome, two storeys up. Who needs windows?

There's white marble everywhere: marble floors, marble columns—even the staircase is marble. A little waterfall bubbles down bush rock into a marble pool at the foot of the stairs. And rising up from it is this tree that reaches all the way up to the dome.

It's not a real tree. I mean, it's a real *tree* but not a live one.

When the house was being built, Mrs Terzis took a drive

17

in the country and found this huge dead gum tree. She had it cut down and taken to the house on the back of a truck. The builder lifted the whole tree into the living room with a crane.

He stuck its base in a block of concrete so it couldn't fall over and then he put the glass dome over the top of the courtyard. Later, Mrs Terzis hired a guy to sand the whole tree smooth and paint it with varnish. Then a pool was built up around the tree and decorated with bush rock and water plants. Water bubbles down through a heap of rock into the water, like a little waterfall. It sounds crazy but it looks fantastic.

They had a specially heated glasshouse built for their orchid collection on the other side of the stairs. Lots of the orchids are from the tropics and they need warm, wet conditions so their little rooty-pooties don't get freezie-weezied.

The tropical fish Mr T wanted to keep need wet conditions too, so Mr T had a special open tank built as a divider between the kitchen and the dining room areas. It's only small—Mr T's idea of small, that is. A white pointer shark could get tired doing laps in it.

And that isn't all.

There's an indoor pool for people, too. Big, beautiful, heated, with a spa and a sauna and changing rooms and all. Plus a small gym. There's also a billiard room and a room they called 'the theatre'. It's got a high density TV with a screen as tall as I am, and a movie projector—a big one like in real movie theatres.

I tell you, the place is a palace. No wonder Mr T doesn't want to go on holiday. He's got everything he wants at home.

Lots of people think Mr and Mrs Terzis were crazy to spend so much money on their house. They reckon the Castle is weird, and that the Terzises would never get their money back if they tried to sell it. But if anyone says that out loud, Mr T just laughs.

'For one, why should we sell?' he says. 'And for the other, this is our home. We please no-one but ourselves here. Right, Anna?'

Mrs T smiles. She adores Mr T, though sometimes he drives her crazy.

'That Stephanos,' my mother always sighs to my father after we've visited Terzis Castle. 'He is *impossible*, Demetrios! The most stubborn man alive. And the money he spends! How Anna copes with him I do not know.'

'Stephanos is—Stephanos,' Dad says, grinning. And Mum shakes her head, but she smiles too.

The fact is, Mr T might be strange in some ways, but people like him. They like Anna Terzis, too. They can't help liking people who are so friendly.

Dad really admires Mr T. Before the emerald robbery he was always telling me what a great example for me his old friend was. 'Work hard like Stephanos, Nick,' he'd say. 'And don't be afraid to take risks.' Then he'd think about it for a second. 'But not too many,' he'd add. 'Stephanos—maybe—takes too many risks.'

Yeah. Like carrying precious stones home in his pocket and keeping them in the safe without proper insurance. You'd think Mr T would have learnt after last time.

But like Mum says, he's a very stubborn man.

4

The scene of
the crime

Where was I?

Oh, yes. Back at the scene of the crime.

After a few minutes Mr T had recovered enough for Liz
and I to help him out of the pond and into a chair. He was
shivering, so I ran upstairs and got a rug and put it around his
shoulders.

'The emeralds,' he groaned. He put his face in his hands
and started rocking backwards and forwards. Pedro and
Pepita, who hadn't left him for a minute, whined and leant
against his legs. I'd noticed Pedro was limping. Looked like
he'd got in the masked man's way once too often.

'It's okay, Mr Terzis,' I said. 'The police are chasing the
car now. They'll get the guy.' But I have to admit, I wasn't so
sure.

He wasn't so sure either. He just mumbled something and
went on rocking.

It was really bad seeing Mr Terzis like this. He was a tough guy. He wasn't afraid of anything. But here he was, soaking wet, wrapped in a blanket, looking like a beaten old man.

He turned to me and said something in Greek. This was strange, because he usually talked to me in English. I guess it was shock. Anyway, I understood him. He wanted me to get some ice for the lump on his forehead.

'Sure, Mr T,' I said. I figured it couldn't do any harm. The ambulance would be arriving any time now, anyway.

I left him and walked carefully on the wet, slippery marble towards the back of the house. I hadn't heard Mr T's story then, but you could tell that the thief had run this way. There was a clear trail of water from the pool, through the dining room, to the kitchen and the back door.

I got the ice from the freezer and wrapped it in a tea towel. I looked around. Everything was so still and peaceful that it was eerie. The refrigerator whirred softly. The fish in their tank swam in circles. The light on the answering machine by the phone blinked gently. Only the water and blood on the floor showed what had happened here.

I looked at the blood. It started at the end of the kitchen space, around where a shallow step led up to the dining area, and tracked on from there. The man in the mask had fallen, then, running on the slippery floor. I squinted at the marks. There were some actual footprints among them. Human footprints, mixed with tiny paw prints.

I squeezed the ice in my hand and fought down the excitement that rose in my chest. Footprints. They'd help

21

identify the thief if necessary. Well, that was something. I skirted the footprints carefully and went back into the living room, rehearsing what I'd say to the cops.

'The guy's footprints are all over the kitchen floor,' I'd say. 'We've kept away from them.'

I gave Mr T his icepack and told him about the footprints, too. He didn't seem too excited, but Liz rushed off with Tom and Richelle to look.

The ambulance turned up. The guys wanted to take Mr T to the hospital, but he wouldn't go. He made them patch him up right there. Made us look pretty silly, but the ambulance guys just accepted what Mr T said and went on their way, smiling. They even checked Pedro's sore leg before they went, to make sure it wasn't broken. Mr T has a way of making people do what he wants, and like it.

A couple of cops turned up then, with Sunny and Elmo. I told them about the footprints, and they seemed quite interested. Not fascinated, mind you. But interested.

The getaway car hadn't been caught yet, but they said all the squad cars had been radioed to be on the lookout for a green station wagon, driving fast. That had been about as much as we could tell them. No licence number. No driver description. Not much of a description of the passenger, either.

Great witnesses we turned out to be.

Of course, guys who wear their pantihose on their heads aren't easy to describe. I suppose that's the point. We all agreed that he was very big. But that was about all we could say.

Then they asked about his clothes. Liz, Tom, Elmo, Sunny and I looked blank. But Richelle brightened up. When you're talking clothes you're on Richelle's home ground. She said that the man in the mask was wearing a black Alezis d'Alpine tracksuit and white Rockland sport shoes. Trust Richelle to be checking designer labels in the middle of a major felony.

'The shoes had red streaks on them,' she said. 'They'd have been better plain.'

'Red streaks?' the policewoman asked. 'Could they have been bloodstains?'

'Oh, yeah,' said Richelle. 'You could be right.'

'I think he had bad concussion,' Sunny said suddenly.

'Why do you think that?'

'He was making all these weird noises. You couldn't understand a word he was saying. Last month one of the girls fell off the rings in gym class and hit her head. She started babbling on just like this guy. It turned out she had concussion.'

We waited near the waterfall pool while two of the police took Mr T's statement. He sat there, with Pedro and Pepita taking turns to lick his hand, and told about how the guy got in, the things he seemed to know about the house, the chase. He didn't mention the gun, I noticed. It was still lying at the bottom of the pool. I didn't touch it. Knowing Mr T, it probably wasn't licensed. I didn't want to get him in more trouble.

Then he told about the emeralds the thief had taken.

Five big, uncut stones. Given to him by an old client, a sheik who wanted Mr T to cut them personally and make them into a necklace for his favourite wife. Even I did a double take when he said what they were worth. That much? For something you chipped out of the ground?

'Insured, of course?' asked the cop taking the statement.

I knew the answer, but the others gasped when Mr T shook his head. No insurance, he said. Not for stones. Not here. The insurance company wouldn't cover me. Not after last time. Then he told them about last year's robbery. The rubies. The cops looked at each other and took notes.

Elmo watched the whole thing like it was a movie he'd saved up a year's allowance to see, and kept shushing us whenever anyone tried to say anything.

'What's up with you, Elmo?' Sunny demanded, in the end.

'He's getting a scoop for the *Pen*,' I said. 'Elmo Zimmer, boy reporter.' I didn't even try to keep the sneer out of my voice.

Elmo's newshound act doesn't usually bother me. After all, his father owns the *Pen*, and it figures that Elmo does what he can to keep the business going. But this time I thought he could have held off. This wasn't just some tacky story. It was a real tragedy. Involving someone I knew.

After a few minutes they'd finished. Mr Terzis was looking better now, but one side of his face was so swollen that it was beginning to look like the winning pumpkin at the Easter Show.

A police officer wrote down our names and addresses.

'You kids can go now,' she said. 'If we need anything else we'll be in touch.'

We were on our way out when another cop came in, talking on his mobile radio.

'They've found the car,' he told the others. 'Smashed into a tree out by the old cemetery. Good place for our man—he's dead.'

'Dead?' Mr Terzis struggled to his feet. 'Have you—?'

'He was the only one in the car, and the emeralds weren't on him, sir,' the cop said. 'The crash killed him. Or finished him off, if he was as badly smashed up when he left here as you say. Looks like the driver's got the stuff off him and done a runner.'

Mr Terzis didn't say anything. He just put his head in his hands. He was trembling all over. I thought he might have been crying but I wasn't sure.

As we left, we saw Mrs Terzis come driving up, jump out of her car and run towards the house. I didn't go back. I couldn't face her.

25

5

All mixed up

'One minute he's walking around and the next minute he's dead,' Tom said. 'I can't believe it. Dead. Gone. Never coming back. He'll never eat another meal or watch TV or anything. He'll never talk to his friends.' Tom shook his head.

It was typical of him that he'd start rabbiting on about some dead crim, when the real point was that Mr Terzis had practically no chance now of getting his emeralds back. That was the real tragedy as far as I was concerned. The guy in the stocking mask meant nothing to me. He'd taken his chances and he'd lost out.

'I still can't believe it,' muttered Liz.

We were walking home. We were all kind of in a state of shock, I guess.

One by one, the gang turned off to go to their houses. Finally it was just Liz and Richelle and me.

'I'm sorry we won't be looking after that house, now,' sighed Richelle after a while. 'It's wonderful.'

'Actually, I don't like it very much,' said Liz. 'I don't

want to insult your parents' friends or anything, Nick, but it's sort of weird. No proper windows. That dead tree in the pool. And the orchids trapped in that glass room. And the fish in the kitchen swimming around and around to nowhere. And all that space, and the marble and everything. It's too cold. Too quiet.'

'Like you wouldn't want to live there,' I jeered.

'No, of course I wouldn't,' she said, staring at me. 'Who would?'

'Come on, Liz, pull the other one.' I couldn't believe this.

'She means it,' nodded Richelle. 'Liz is strange like that. She likes mess, and old stuff, and lots of colours, like at her house. But I think she's crazy. I'd *adore* to live in Terzis Castle. I'd just adore it.'

We walked along for about half a block without talking. I didn't feel like it. I couldn't get the picture out of my mind of Mr T sitting there with his head in his hands.

'Why on earth didn't Mr Terzis have insurance?' Liz asked finally.

'Didn't you hear what he told the cops?' I said. 'He was robbed last June. Someone broke in and blew the safe open while he was still at work and Mrs T was playing cards. Come to think about it, that means that robbery was on a Friday too. Mrs T always plays cards on a Friday. I guess someone knows that.'

'A lot of people must know,' said Liz. 'Didn't the neighbours hear the explosion?'

'No, the walls are too thick.'

'What did they lose that time?'

'Rubies. Uncut stones. Mr T had only brought them home the day before. He was going to cut them in his workroom. Like with the emeralds. He likes doing that with important stones.' I smiled. 'You know, he carries them home loose in his pocket.'

'That's crazy!' Richelle put in.

I shrugged. 'Not so crazy. Mr T reckons it's safer that way. When they're uncut, they just look like bits of rock. If he just carries stones in his pocket, no-one needs to know he's got them. But if he heaves round, say, a briefcase chained to his wrist, everyone will know he's carrying something valuable home. See?'

Liz nodded, but she looked a bit doubtful. 'Someone did know, though, didn't they?' she said. 'This time with the emeralds, and last year with the rubies.'

I didn't say anything. But I had to admit to myself that Mr Terzis's strategy hadn't been what you'd call a great success.

'Why does he want to work on them at home anyway?' said Richelle. 'You'd think he'd want to just relax there. You know, forget all about boring old work. That's what home's for, isn't it?'

I knew it would be pointless to try to explain to Richelle that Mr T adored his work, and would rather cut gemstones than do just about anything else. She'd find that impossible to understand. So I gave her a simple answer. 'He says it's quieter at home.'

'Not today,' murmured Richelle.

I winced. She was right there.

Liz was still worrying away at the insurance problem. 'But I still don't understand why he's not insured,' she argued. 'I mean, what have the rubies got to do with it?'

'The insurance company paid up for the rubies,' I told her patiently. 'But they told Mr T they wouldn't cover another loss at home, or on the way home, unless he did certain things. Like put in one of those alarms that senses people walking through rooms of the house, for example.'

'And he *didn't*?' exclaimed Liz.

'No. He just put in the one that works on the front and back doors. He thought the dogs would be always setting the other sort off. Which they would, I guess. And he reckoned it wasn't necessary anyway because nobody can get in or out of that house except through one of the doors.'

'Let's face it, the insurance people were right, weren't they?' Richelle yawned and stretched.

'How do you mean?'

'Someone did get in.'

'So what? It wouldn't have mattered what kind of alarm system he had. If someone jumps out of the bushes and holds a knife to your throat you're going to do anything the guy says. If he says, "Turn off the alarm", you're going to turn it off, aren't you?'

'I guess you are,' Liz agreed.

'Anybody would,' I said. 'So Mr T wasn't actually wrong. But because he didn't do what the insurance company said, they won't pay up.'

So he's in real trouble, I thought.

'Didn't Mr Terzis say the emeralds belonged to a sheik or something?' Richelle put my thoughts into words. 'He's going to have to pay the sheik back. Lucky he's so rich.'

'Mr T's rich, but not rich enough to pay out that sort of money,' I said slowly. 'This could ruin him.'

'Oh, I had no idea!' exclaimed Liz. 'Oh, this is awful! You mean he might even have to sell his house?'

'What do you care, Liz?' I said. 'I thought you hated the place.'

She flushed red. 'I don't like it much,' she murmured. 'But Mr and Mrs Terzis do. It's their home. I don't like to think of them losing it, that's all.'

'Oh, they'll be all right,' I said, turning away. My thoughts were all mixed up. Liz is a softie. She's always feeling sorry for people and worrying about them. But I'm more realistic than that. Mostly, I reckon, people get what they ask for, and there's no point in them whingeing about it afterwards.

I suppose a lot of people would say that Mr Terzis deserved what he got—taking a risk like that with such valuable stuff. I know I would have said it, if I didn't know him.

But I did know him. And I couldn't imagine him without his house, or his business. I couldn't stand the thought of him losing everything he and Mrs T had built up, because of one mistake. It just seemed so unfair.

Suddenly, instead of feeling mixed up, I started to feel angry.

'If only we'd had the sense to get a good look at the guy driving the car,' I hissed between clenched teeth. 'His mate takes all the risks and ends up dead. He just drives the getaway car and walks off with a fortune. It stinks! And we could have stopped it. But what do we do? Hide in the bushes like a bunch of scared kids.'

Liz and Richelle looked at me like I was crazy.

'We were hiding in the bushes, Nick,' Richelle pointed out, 'because a masked man was waving a knife at us.'

'He wasn't going to do anything,' I said. 'He had concussion. In fact, we probably could've jumped him and got the emeralds back.'

'Nick, you know that would have been stupid.' Liz was watching me carefully. 'We didn't know how badly hurt he was. And no amount of money's worth dying for.'

I shrugged, and turned off to go down to my own street. But I thought about what she'd said. She was right, of course. No amount of money's worth dying for. Yet one man had died.

Had he known that his plan to steal the Terzis emeralds could end like that? Had the driver of the getaway car known? Probably not. They hadn't counted on Mr Terzis putting up a fight.

I must have been feeling weak—maybe it was the shock, or maybe I'd fallen under Liz's influence during the walk home. Because suddenly I started thinking about the thieves

31

as people instead of straight rip-off merchants. Were they friends? Was the driver of the getaway car upset that the other guy had been killed? Or was he pleased, because now he wouldn't have to share the money the emeralds would bring with anyone else?

We'd never know. Unless by some miracle the cops could find him. And the emeralds.

That brought me back to the real world. The emeralds. They were the important thing. The emeralds. And Mr Terzis. I frowned, staring down at the cracked footpath. I raked through my memory. My memory was usually very good. There must be some detail I'd noticed that would help. Some clue I could give the cops.

I came up with zilch. I tried again. I went over and over it. Nothing.

I could feel my hands balling into fists, and made myself relax. No point in getting het up. Cool thinking was what was needed here.

There had to be something I could do to help. There had to be.

6

Getting nowhere fast

'Nicko! Nicko!' Mum screamed. 'Are you all right?'

The news had spread like fleas at a dog show. By the time I got home, Mum had moved into hyper-panic mode.

'I'm all right. I'm all right,' I said. 'Look at me. Don't I look okay? Hey, Mum, lay off. You're crushing my shirt.'

'Oh, Nicko!'

Nothing I said was going to calm her down. She just kept hugging me and kissing me like I'd just come back from a suicide mission to Mars.

'Ma,' I said, 'it's okay. He didn't do anything to us.'

'He could have killed you!' she wailed. 'He could have stuck you with that knife.'

'Yeah, but he didn't. Okay?'

You could tell that Dad had been worried about me too. But Dad doesn't like to show it. He's the strong, silent type. He concentrated on Stephanos.

'Only last night I was telling Stephanos it was stupidity to have brought those stones to his home,' he said. 'I was there when he got in. Roses for Anna, a fortune in emeralds in his pocket with the loose change. I told him it was madness. He wouldn't listen to me. Or to Anna. And now, you see.'

He picked up the phone and punched in the number of the Terzis house.

'Poor Anna,' my mother whispered. 'She is desperate. The house—if the emeralds are not found, they're going to have to sell the house! And Stephanos won't see the doctor. His face, Nicko—she says his face is all bashed on one side. And Pedro has such a painful leg, poor little baby—Nicko, you can't imagine—'

'Mum, I was just there,' I said.

'Hello, Anna. It's me, Demetrios,' said my father into the phone. 'Yes, he's home. He's fine. Okay, we'll be right over.'

That night I was in my room trying to forget about Terzis Castle, the emeralds, and everything else. I was trying to blot it out by concentrating on this new computer game Elmo Zimmer had lent me.

Unfortunately, he'd lost the instruction book. I had it two days and I still hadn't worked it out.

It was called *Escape from Zargos* and it must have had a million rules. None of which I knew. All I knew was I was in a dungeon with all these doors. That's where you start, and that's where I'd stayed. I couldn't get out of that rotten dungeon no matter what I did. I'd worked out how to move the little hero around from door to door, but that was about all.

As soon as you get to a door there's this scrambled message. You have to work out what it says. If you get it wrong a dwarf whips out of the door and cuts your head off with an axe. No second chances. Every time I tried a new door, my guy's head ended up eating dirt and I had to start all over again.

Anyway, I could have rung Elmo and asked him about it, but the idea didn't appeal to me. I'm supposed to be the computer games hot-shot. I shouldn't need help. Especially from Elmo. So every time I picked up the phone to call I'd end up hanging up. Somehow it seemed better to keep getting my head cut off.

I got beheaded again, gave up and went and lay on my bed, still puzzling about the robbery. I'd drawn a blank on remembering anything about the driver of the car. So I'd decided to think about the case from another angle. From the beginning.

The emeralds were safe in the shop because there were surveillance cameras all over the place. You couldn't rob Mr T there without your face ending up in the newspapers. But his home was different. No cameras.

Someone crooked knew he'd taken them home. But who?

Mr T was a pretty careful guy. He wasn't about to start telling the world when he was toting a fortune around in his pocket.

I counted off on my fingers the people who must have known. Mrs Terzis would have known. She'd probably tried to persuade him not to do it, too. She was scared after the theft of the rubies. I remembered that. But she'd hardly send in a thug with a knife to steal the emeralds. The Terzises had been married something like twenty years. So she was out.

I gathered from what Dad had said that he'd known, but I knew he wouldn't steal the emeralds. For one thing, Mr T was his oldest friend. For another thing, Dad just wouldn't. He might be a smart operator in business, but he wouldn't take a cent that he didn't think belonged to him.

Miles Silvestro, Mr T's assistant, would have known. Could he have done it? He was a boring, fussy sort of guy, but that didn't mean he was honest, did it?

Of course Miles had worked for Mr T for years. Practically ran the business now, in many ways. But that didn't really mean anything either. He could still have decided to make a killing on his own account. If he had a fortune, he wouldn't need to work ever again, would he?

I tossed my head on the pillow. Miles? But Miles was so—ordinary. It just didn't seem likely that he'd mastermind a plan involving knives and getaway cars.

So where did that leave me? Nowhere. I jumped off the bed and went back to *Escape from Zargos*. I got to a door, tried to work out the message, and lost my head. Again. Great.

My parents came back late. I was still trying to work out *Escape from Zargos*. When I heard them at the door, I quickly exited from the game but left the computer on.

'Better get to sleep, Nick,' My father said, poking his head around the door.

'How's Mr T?' I asked.

'Not so good,' Dad said. 'The police still haven't found a

trace of the driver of the car. There's no word about the emeralds either. Poor Stephanos.' He shook his head.

'What if the cops told all the dealers in Australia to be on the lookout for the stones?' I asked.

'Stephanos is sure they'll be smuggled overseas and cut there,' Dad said. 'Think how easy that would be, Nicko. Someone catches a plane, all innocent, and in their pocket five little pebbles. Who would know?'

'So what's he going to do?' I asked.

'What can he do? He'll have to sell up.' Dad frowned. 'As you know, Nicko, I'd give him anything I had. I told him that tonight. Your mother did too. But I couldn't raise a quarter of what he needs.'

'Bye 'bye business. Mr Terzis had spent his whole life making sure people got a good deal from him and looking for those special customers who'd pay a lot of money to get exactly the quality they wanted. 'Bye 'bye sheik. 'Bye 'bye Terzis Castle.

'Demetrios,' Mum said, bustling into the room, 'you will be making Nicko sad. This isn't good for him just before sleep.'

Her eyes were red as if she'd been crying. But she smiled at me and started fussing with my bed, turning it down just like she used to do when I was a little kid.

'This will make you happy, Nicko,' she chattered on. 'Anna and Stephanos are going on holiday anyway. Robbery or no robbery. They want you and your friends to look after the house. The six of you, all together, so you'll be quite safe.'

'Really?' I stood up. This was a real surprise.

'Anna put her foot down. She told Stephanos that they

need the holiday now more than ever. And how can he go to work all bashed up? So they leave Monday, as planned.'

'Great,' I said. But I wasn't all that pleased, really. Somehow the idea of looking after Terzis Castle had lost its appeal. The place was sort of sad, now, instead of fabulous. I guess it was because the Terzises were about to lose it.

'Anna wants you to come to her tomorrow so she can explain everything,' Mum went on. 'She says not to worry about bringing the others this time. She knows your friends must be nice boys and girls. Okay?'

'Sure, Ma.'

She pursed her lips. 'Now, Nicko, you will be responsible,' she warned. 'You tell Liz and Tom and the others no playing around in Anna's house. This is a very big responsibility.'

'No sweat, responsible is my middle name. Nick Responsible Kontellis. It has a certain ring . . .'

'What are you talking about?' Mum said. She looked at the computer and shook her head. 'And stop playing with that thing.'

'What makes you think I'm playing? I might be writing an essay for school!'

'Nicko,' she said, 'look at me. I'm your mum, remember?'

'I almost forgot.'

'Turn that thing off and get to bed before you get cancer of the eyes.'

'Everybody has to die of something, Ma.'

'Oh, Nicko!'

7

The job

Next day Dad bought all the papers. Every one carried a story about the robbery, and every one managed to get something wrong.

One of them said that we—the Teen Power gang, that is—were collecting for a charity when we 'interrupted a robbery in progress'. One said there were four of us, another five, and another six.

Mr Terzis was Stephen Terazza and Stephano Terza and even Pedro Merzis. His age was somewhere between sixty and seventy-two and he was from everywhere from Greece to Greenland. He'd been wounded with a knife and rushed to hospital. He'd been beaten about the head and left for dead, and kicked in the leg. His wife of twenty years, thirty years and forty years, Anna, Anya and Agnes, was at his bedside.

Where they really had fun was telling how much the emeralds were worth. One said two million. Another one said four-and-a-half million. Another one said 'maybe as much as six million'. The smaller the newspaper, the bigger the amount of money.

'Why do the newspapers get everything wrong?' Mum asked. 'Whenever they write about something you know, you can see it. Everything wrong. Even your friend Elmo's newspaper is always wrong.'

'I try not to tell him that,' I said. 'It hurts his feelings.'

The police still didn't know who the dead man was, but the owner of the getaway car had been traced. She was a schoolteacher from Avon Heights, and she'd reported the car stolen from a supermarket car park only a couple of hours before the robbery. So that lead was a dead end, too.

In fact, everywhere you looked there were dead ends.

I went over to Terzis Castle around two that afternoon.

Mrs Terzis peeped out through the peephole before opening the door. You weren't supposed to be able to see someone looking out, but you could. In fact, if I'd seen her eyeball any better I could have written her a prescription for glasses.

When I got inside she carefully turned the key in the deadlock again, sealing us inside. The Terzises weren't risking any more unexpected visitors.

'I have written everything down on a list for you, Nick,' she said, handing over a sheaf of papers covered with handwriting. 'And you know the house. So as I told Stephanos, everything will be fine.'

She sounded as if she was trying to convince herself. I tried to look confident and reassuring. She smiled at me nervously, and patted my arm.

'Here is a spare key,' she burbled, handing it over. 'Don't lose it, all right? And don't give it to anyone else. Only you keep it. There are no more gems in the house, but Stephanos worries about the paintings and furniture and things. You know how he is.'

I knew. 'Gotcha, Mrs T.'

'After the burglary we have changed the number to turn off the alarm. The new number is 4565. Can you remember that?'

'4565. 4565. 4565,' I mumbled. 'Got it.'

'The police say that from your description, Nick, the man who attacked Stephanos had bad concussion. He probably could not speak to the man who drove the car. So it is unlikely he tell him the alarm numbers. But still, we take no chances. Turn the alarm off with those numbers when you come in, and don't forget to set it again when you go.'

'Okay.'

'Oh, and please tell your friends, excuse the mess. I will have no time to get the cleaners in again before we leave. I do not clean any of the upstairs before we go. Only the downstairs. Pretend you blind,' she added, putting a hand over her eyes and laughing.

Mrs Terzis's idea of mess was a magazine on the floor or a fingerprint on a vase. She'd probably never seen the average kid's bedroom. She'd probably never waded through toys up to her ankles, picked chewing gum out of a carpet or peeled a half-eaten peanut butter sandwich off a skirting board. She had no idea.

'I'm sure the mess won't bother us,' I said. 'By the way, how's Mr T? Is he all right?'

'He worry himself sick. The older he gets the more he worry anyhow. And then this happen to us.' Mrs Terzis put up her palms and gave a what-can-you-do shrug. 'He is lying down now. He go to work this morning for one hour and straightaway he have fight with Miles. Poor Miles, what he puts up with.'

She wrinkled her nose. 'Stephanos does not want to go away on this holiday,' she said loudly. Maybe she was hoping Mr T would overhear. 'But it will do him good. Make him less like an angry bear, maybe.'

I decided to get back to business. I looked at the list she'd given me. List? It was more like a series of essays on the subject of expensive house care.

'Fish,' I muttered, scanning the little headings Mrs T had underlined in red at the top of each page. 'Orchids. Birds. Fish. Pool. Sprinkler system. Dusting. Mail. Answering machine . . . What about Pedro and Pepita?'

Mrs T looked shocked. 'Oh, Pedro and Pepita are coming with us,' she exclaimed. 'Didn't you know that? Oh, Nick, no way Stephanos and I could leave our babies here, alone.'

Well, that was a relief, anyway. Pedro and Pepita were cute little dogs, but I must say I'd been a bit nervous about having to look after them. They probably ate chicken breast, cut up fine, with wine sauce and parsley on the top. And what if they choked on a stalk, or something? They were so small.

'We'll start on Tuesday after school. Is that okay?' I asked her.

Mrs Terzis smiled and nodded.

'Sure,' she said. 'And you help yourself to food and drink, all right, Nick? I know how you kids like to eat. I have left the refrigerator full. It is not worth emptying it for one week. You and your friends take what you need.'

'Thanks, Mrs T.' I wondered if she knew what she was saying. If I let Tom loose on the Terzis's fridge it'd be picked clean in an afternoon.

Mrs Terzis turned the key in the deadlock and opened the front door to let me out. But then she got a last-minute attack of nerves. She put her hand back on my arm.

'You will be very careful, Nick, won't you?' she whispered. No way she wanted Mr T to overhear her now. 'You come together to the house, you and your friends. Look after each other. And you don't let anybody in, all right? Nobody. I promised Stephanos. And you will be careful with the key, and the alarm—and the orchids, and—'

'Don't you worry about a thing, Mrs T,' I said. Nick Responsible Kontellis. 'Just have a good time. Everything will be okay, really. Trust me.'

She looked at me doubtfully. No wonder. I sounded like a used car salesman, even to myself.

I walked on home telling myself everything was going to be fine.

Sure the house was big and expensive and full of white rugs, expensive machinery, delicate tropical fish and orchids that fell over as soon as anyone breathed too hard in their direction. Sure the owners would have heart attacks if anything living died, or anything already dead got broken or marked.

Sure I was about to expose this house to my friends.

Why was I worried?

Didn't I trust my friends?

I took a deep breath and abandoned that line of thought. I began thinking about *Escape From Zargos* instead. It was much safer.

8

A little piece of
heaven

Tuesday.

School was finished for the day.

All the Teen Power kids except Sunny were standing outside Terzis Castle. I studied the note that listed Mrs T's instructions about getting into the house.

'Where's Sunny?' I asked.

'Probably at gym or something,' Liz said. 'She didn't say she was going. Maybe she forgot.'

'Okay, step number one,' I said. 'Tom, could you check out the bushes?'

'They're great,' he said, nodding. 'I love them. Where can I buy some just like them?'

Tom never passes up an opportunity to make a joke. And there's no joke too weak, too corny to keep to himself. Bad for the image, Tom, I often think. But you can't tell him anything.

I raised my eyebrow at him. He grinned back. He looked more like an oddball today than usual. He was wearing an enormous overcoat that looked as if it was second-hand when his grandpa bought it, and this old knitted scarf that wound around and around his neck and trailed down his back. He really irritated me.

'Just have a look around in them, will you?' I said.

'How about a reason, Nick?'

'Because that's what it says on the note,' I snapped. 'Oh, never mind.'

I had a quick look through the bushes myself. No lurking robbers. All clear.

'The guy is gone, Nick,' Tom said. 'He's dead, remember?'

'Tom,' I muttered, 'just shut up.'

I put the key in the lock and opened the front door. Everyone went into the house. I pulled the door shut quickly and felt better once the lock clicked into place.

'Maybe we should have a swim before we start work,' Richelle said. 'Or a spa.'

'Hang on, Richelle,' I said. 'Don't talk for a second. I've got to get the code into the keypad otherwise we'll be up to our armpits in police.'

4564. That was it.

I half-covered the key pad with one hand so no-one could see it and then punched the numbers in. Out of the corner of my eye I saw Tom pointing at me and pretending to double over with silent laughter. He was being a real pain.

It took me two goes to get it right but, finally, the green

light came on. I breathed out for the first time.

'Okay,' I said. 'We're in.'

Richelle went spinning into the living room like a dancer, her arms out and her face turned up towards the dome.

'Oh, it's so gorgeous!' she sang. 'Oh, it's *heaven*. Oh, I want this house. I need it. I *have* to have it!'

'Okay, gang,' I said, shuffling through the notes. 'Here are your orders: Tom, you turn on the lawn sprinklers—controls near the back door—and feed the fish.'

'What fish?'

'In the kitchen. Through that arch over there,' I said, pointing and handing him the notes. 'Just read these, and follow what they say exactly.'

'Lighten up, Nick,' grinned Tom. He'd pulled off his overcoat, but left the scarf on. Of course. He wouldn't want to look normal.

'I'm light, I'm light. If I was any lighter I'd be floating.'

Tom took the note and wandered off to the kitchen to find the fish food.

'Richelle,' I said. 'How would you like to water the plants?'

'In the glasshouse?'

'That's the place. Mrs Terzis took all the plants in the house and put them in there. All you have to do is turn on the water—if you can figure out how.'

Richelle gave me a dirty look.

'I mean it's not easy,' I said. 'There's a sprinkler system.

47

Some pipes spray and other ones drip. There are all these valves and things. The controls are on the outside, behind a metal panel near the door. There's a diagram on the note but it's tricky, okay?'

'Sure.' She took her note and went off towards the glasshouse.

That left Elmo, Liz and me.

'What's it going to be?' I asked. 'Dusting, or feeding the birds?'

Liz shuddered. 'I hate birds in cages,' she said. 'It's cruel.'

'Well it won't help to let them starve to death,' I snapped.

'I'll dust,' said Liz, holding out her hand. 'Though how there can be any dust after one day I don't know.'

I gave her the note headed 'Dusting'. She went off reading it and sighing like the troubles of the world's birds were on her personal shoulders.

I handed Elmo his instructions. 'You're elected as birdman, Zimmer. Congratulations.'

I didn't have to tell him where the birds were. Suddenly two of the cockatoos started screeching like they'd just got into a bad batch of birdseed. Elmo turned to see the room-sized aviary through a doorway down past the glasshouse.

'The seed is in a can inside the aviary. There's a pile of newspapers just outside.'

'Newspapers? Do they always read when they eat?'

'For the bottom of the cage,' I explained. 'You know, poopsie-woopsie, messy-wessy. Why do you think the Terzises

48

like getting the *Pen*?'

Elmo decided to let my comment about his dad's newspaper go.

'Do I have to go inside the cage?' he asked.

'Let's put it this way—yes.'

'What if they peck me to death?'

'We'll give an exclusive interview to the *Pen*. Think of the headline: OWNER'S SON SLAIN BY PARROTS. That should move a few copies. Now feed the birds. Please?'

'Whatever you say,' Elmo mumbled. He didn't look too pleased.

I crossed the living room and went down the little corridor to the swimming pool. I got the pool chemicals out of their cupboard and started following Mrs T's instructions about adding them to the water.

There was something eerie about the room, something about the way the lights reflected off the water and onto the walls and ceiling, something about the sound of the water lapping in the gutters.

I felt the water. The heat had been turned off but it was still a nice temperature: not too warm, not too cold. Maybe Richelle was right and we should have a swim. That would cheer everyone up no end. Make me a big hero. And the Terzises wouldn't mind. In fact, if we cleaned up afterwards, they'd never know.

Then I looked around the echoing room again. Or maybe it wasn't such a good idea after all. Somehow the deep, lapping pool wasn't very inviting.

49

I finished what I had to do as quickly as I could and went back to the living room. Liz was still dusting. Tom was either still looking for the fish food or—more than likely—skiving off.

At the glasshouse, the metal flap that covered the sprinkler controls was open, but Richelle didn't seem to be around. I opened the door and went in. It was warm and sticky. And down at one end was Richelle, sitting on a plastic chair surrounded by plants and reading a magazine.

'What are you doing, Richelle?' I asked.

She just shrugged.

'Have you watered the plants?' I looked around. They didn't look watered to me.

'Not yet,' she said dreamily. 'I've set the controls and everything. Just have to push the button, now. I'll do it in a minute. I just want to read this. It's nice and warm in here. There's plenty of time.'

Liz was dusting the coffee table. Well, she had a dusting cloth in her hand, but what she was actually doing when I came up to her was looking at the card that stood in front of the vase filled with red roses.

'You read Greek,' she said. 'What does it say?'

'It says "Happy Thursday, my love".'

Liz looked surprised.

'It's this old thing,' I explained. 'Mr Terzis brings Mrs T flowers every week. When they were first married he used to get paid on Thursdays, and he used to do it then. Even when they hardly had enough money to live, he always bought her flowers. So he still does.'

'Every Thursday he brings her flowers?' Liz's eyes were shining and she had on her soppy look. 'After all these years? Isn't that romantic! Isn't that *lovely*!'

'Lovely for the florist,' I said. 'Mr T probably keeps her in business. Personally, if I was Mrs T, I'd rather have the money.'

'Nick, I want to tell you that you'll make someone a truly horrible husband one day,' said Liz. She turned her back on me to start dusting the vase.

9

Bird brains

Elmo was in the bird house, talking to a galah.

'Hello, Cocky,' he said.

'Hello, Cocky,' the galah said back.

'Hello, Cocky,' said Elmo.

'Hello, Cocky,' said the galah.

'Hello, Cocky,' said Elmo.

I wondered how long this had been going on.

Elmo heard my footsteps and turned his head.

'Hello, Cocky,' said the galah.

'Why does he do it?' Elmo said to me.

'Why did he do what?'

'Why does he keep repeating what I say? I'm serious. I say "Hello, Cocky" over and over and over and he just kept giving it to me right back.'

'Parrots do that, Elmo,' I said patiently. Where had this boy been?

'Yes, but why? I've never thought about it before, but why do they?'

Unfortunately, Elmo has a very serious and—let's be honest—boring side to him.

'Well I don't know, Elmo,' I said. 'Maybe they're just being polite. If you've finished here, how about helping Liz with the dusting?'

'Sure.'

When we passed the glasshouse I could see that Richelle was still sitting down and *still* reading the same magazine. I put my head around the door and called out to her.

'Richelle, I hope you don't expect to get paid for sitting around.'

'Oh, yeah,' she said, vaguely. 'Be with you in a minute.'

I closed the door again and leant against the glass, with Elmo hovering beside me. I counted to ten. This was really stupid. Irritating and stupid. Whatever Mrs Terzis and my mother had decided, having the whole Teen Power gang together in this house was incredibly inefficient.

I watched Liz slowly plumping up an embroidered cushion by the waterfall pool. She didn't usually waste time. But this job encouraged it.

I'd be much better off doing the whole thing myself—or with just one other person. There wasn't enough work for six. Gave everyone too much time to muck around. Something bad was going to happen. I could feel it.

Right on cue a sort of growling noise burst out from the direction of the kitchen. Liz jumped, squeaked and dropped the cushion into the pool. It sank slowly to the bottom.

'Hey!' I shouted in a panic. 'Liz!'

53

'What's that noise?' demanded Elmo, looking spooked.

'The garbage disposal,' I gabbled, watching Liz fishing for the cushion. 'Moysten can't keep his hands off any rotten thing.' I raised my voice. 'Tom, turn that off!' I roared.

Then a few things happened at once.

The growling noise suddenly changed to a sort of choking roar mixed with these weird gurgles and bangs. Liz ran for the kitchen, leaving the cushion to soak. Elmo grabbed my arm. I jerked away from him. My elbow, out of control, hit the glasshouse sprinkler button.

There was an instant cloudburst behind the glass. The whole inside of the glasshouse disappeared in mist. Richelle too. You couldn't see her, but you could hear her. Screeching her head off. The metal cover had fallen down over the sprinkler controls again. I picked at it, but it wouldn't lift.

'Nick!' screamed Liz from the kitchen. 'Oh, Nick, quick. Quick! Tom—'

I knew panic when I heard it. I left Elmo fumbling at the sprinkler control cover, and ran for it. Richelle wouldn't drown for a while, and it sounded as though things were hotting up in the kitchen.

I bolted through the archway to the dining room and looked through to the kitchen area. For a minute I couldn't take in what I was seeing. I guess I couldn't believe it. I couldn't believe anyone would be so stupid.

Tom was bent over the sink. Over the garbage disposal hole, to be exact. He didn't look very happy. His face was bright red. His eyes were popping. His hands were clutched at his throat. One end of his scarf was disappearing into the garbage disposal. The rest of it was wound around his neck, choking him. He couldn't get it loose. With his face in the sink he couldn't reach the other end of the scarf, hanging down his back. And the wool around his throat was tightening more every second.

The garbage disposal roared away, swallowing up more and more of the stripy wool. A bit of a change for it from potato peelings and chip packets, I guess. A few more minutes and it would get Tom as well as his scarf.

Liz was screaming, dancing around, trying to unwind the scarf to give Tom air. But it was hopeless. He was struggling and thrashing around so much, and the scarf was so twisted up, that she couldn't do anything.

'Liz! The switch! Turn off the switch!' I yelled.

She looked around in panic. I dived through the dining room into the kitchen, stumbling down the shallow step and nearly falling into the fish tank on the way. I reached the sink and punched the garbage disposal button. Instantly, the roaring stopped.

The silence was deafening.

Tom heaved, and groaned.

'Stand still, you idiot!' I snarled between gritted teeth. I held him while Liz, shaking like she was freezing, unwound the scarf. It was wound around his neck about three times. No wonder she hadn't been able to do it before.

Finally, he was free. He straightened up and staggered back from the sink. He pointed to the garbage disposal. 'It tried to strangle me,' he croaked. 'It's evil.'

'It was only doing its job,' I said coldly. 'Who asked you to turn it on, anyway? I hope you haven't broken it.'

'Nick, Tom could have been *killed*!' Liz yelled. 'How can you—?'

She stopped. 'What's that?' she asked.

I'd been wondering when she'd notice the screaming and crying going on in the living room.

I sighed. 'Follow me,' I said, and trudged back to face Richelle.

She was standing outside the glasshouse, streaming with water. Her hair was plastered to her head and dripping down her back. She looked like something washed up on a beach. She was screaming hysterically. Elmo was standing well back, staring, with his mouth open.

Liz started to laugh. And I had to admit, it was a funny sight. I might have smiled myself. In fact I think I must have, because Richelle suddenly stopped screaming. Her eyes disappeared into slits. And then she came at me, splashing and sliding on the marble floor. Before I could jump back, she'd kicked me right in the shins. Very hard.

'Hey! Stop that!' I yelled, grabbing my leg. 'What are you doing?'

'Serves you right for soaking me! You did it on purpose!'

'I did not! It was a complete accident!'

'Oh, yeah?' she said, stomping away. 'Well, that kick was a complete accident, too. Hope it hurt. A lot.'

I rubbed at my leg. It did hurt. A lot. Richelle is stronger than she looks. All that ballet dancing she does has given her leg muscles like a carthorse.

Liz laughed even harder. I scowled at her. Sometimes Liz goes too far.

'I'm leaving!' shrilled Richelle, splashing over the marble towards the front door. 'You can finish this stupid job all on your own!'

'Richelle,' gasped Liz, between giggles. 'You can't go home like that. You'll freeze to death.'

'You watch me,' screamed Richelle. 'You just watch me. I don't care if I die of pneumonia. It would serve you all right!'

She turned into the entrance hall. I gloomily surveyed the trail of water she'd left behind her. More cleaning up. At this rate I'd be in the house all night.

'Hey!' Richelle's voice shrieked. 'Nick! You deadhead! Unlock the door!'

A strange feeling swam into my stomach. Unlock the door?

I limped across the living room with the others following me. Richelle was standing by the front door, shivering and frowning furiously. I tried to turn the handle. It wouldn't budge. The door was deadlocked.

Stupid me, I thought, shaking my head to clear it. That's the way it's supposed to be. You need the key to get out.

I searched in my pockets for the key. No key.

Where was it? What had I done with it? I looked around the entrance to the glasshouse to see if it had dropped out of my pocket when Richelle kicked me. Nothing.

I turned to the others. 'Would any of you know where the front door key is?' I asked carefully.

'I do,' Tom said. He was rubbing at his throat, but even so that silly grin was starting to spread over his face again.

'Then give it to me, you idiot,' I yelled at him.

He wagged his finger at me. 'I didn't say I *had* it. I said I know where it is,' he said. 'Or at least, I have my suspicions.'

I stared at him, trying to wear him down, but he just grinned on and said nothing. I felt like hitting him. And then, only then, a horrible thought occurred to me.

I couldn't remember taking the key out of the lock after I opened the door. I couldn't remember bringing it inside. And that meant . . .

'Oh, Nick!' yelled Liz. 'You've left the key in the door! On the outside!'

'Great security,' Elmo commented. 'We can't get out, but anybody who wants to can get in.'

'We're trapped!' Richelle stamped her soggy foot. 'Okay, mastermind, what are we going to do?'

'I'm thinking,' I said. 'I'm thinking.'

'Richelle,' Liz said, seizing her chance. 'Why don't you go and find a towel and dry off while we sort this out? In fact, if you give me your wet clothes I'll put them in the dryer for you. There's plenty of time. Now.' She paused. 'You know, you'd look really silly going out in the street like that,' she added.

Liz knows Richelle. They haven't been friends since pre-school for nothing. Richelle thought for a moment, then nodded and wandered up the stairs, squelching as she went. There were a couple of bathrooms downstairs, but she wasn't going to miss an opportunity to play rich ladies upstairs. Not for anything.

10

Trapped

How were we going to get out of there? Easy. Like Liz said, when she came back from putting Richelle's clothes in the dryer. We'd just have to ring someone and get them to come over and open the door. But who?

Elmo said we should ring the cops. No, I said, we didn't want to get the police involved.

Liz wanted me to ring my parents.

'And have them tell Mr and Mrs T? No way. I don't want them finding out that we locked ourselves in.'

'You mean, *you* locked us in,' said Tom. 'How about ringing one of the neighbours? I think I know the name of the lady across the street. We could just look her up in the phone book.'

'Same problem,' I said. 'She'll spill the beans. How about your mother, Liz? She'd keep her mouth shut, wouldn't she?'

Liz shook her head. 'No,' she said. 'I mean, yes, she wouldn't say anything. But she's no good. She won't be home till seven tonight. Some thing at the bank. And Dad's working late too.'

'I could ring my mother,' said Tom. 'She can keep a secret.'

'That's no go,' I reminded him. 'You're forgetting about Brian. He'd tell the world. He'd think it was his duty.'

Tom's mother is fine, but he has this really boring stepfather, Brian Murphy. He's an ancient history teacher at Raven Hill High, and we all know him. I admit that having Tom as a stepson would be my idea of hell, but having Brian as a stepfather would be even worse.

Sometimes my parents get me down, fussing and so on. But they go along with me, mostly, and don't give me a hard time. So now and again I feel quite sorry for Tom. He sends up Brian all the time, and jokes about him. But it can't be much fun living with a pig like that.

'Brian's not coming home till late tonight,' Tom grinned. 'The coast is clear.' He puffed out his chest. 'Behold your saviour!'

Liz and Elmo cheered. I scowled. But any saviour was better than none at all. Of course I had to agree that he should make the call.

So now Tom was Mr Wonderful. And he started making the most of it in typical fashion. He cruised back through the house and into the kitchen, with us trailing behind him. Then he said his throat was still sore, and insisted on getting a Coke from the fridge to soothe it.

It wasn't the first he'd taken, I realised. There was already an empty can on the sink. But I didn't say anything, and in the end we all got a drink. I thought I could do with a lift.

The second Tom reached for the phone disaster struck. Nothing in the Terzis house was ordinary. And the phone was no exception. It had a complete keyboard. It was a fax and phone and computer all rolled into one.

Now picture Tom reaching out to pick up the receiver. Naturally, being Tom, he used the hand with the can of Coke in it. Naturally, being Tom, he was so busy grinning and playing up to his audience that he didn't watch what he was doing.

You guessed it: the Coke can tipped. A stream of brown liquid dripped into the phone. There was a crack, and the smell of burning. Tom dropped the can and leapt backwards.

'Ouch!' he yelled, jamming his fingers into his mouth. 'I got a shock.'

I grabbed a wad of tissues from a box on the bench and dried the phone. Then I picked up the receiver. There wasn't even a crackle.

'You've shorted it out,' I shouted. 'Moysten you—'

'Stupid thing bit me,' he mumbled. 'The machines in this house are out to get me. Ow, ow—it hurts!'

I left Liz and Elmo inspecting his hand. It looked fine to me, just a bit pink. But Mr Wonderful was carrying on as though it was a charred stump. I gritted my teeth and went to find another phone.

There were about half a dozen in Terzis Castle, and every one of them was stone dead, even the one in the workroom. Tom had successfully destroyed the whole system. As I limped past one of the bathrooms upstairs I heard the taps running in the bath. Richelle was locked in there, singing softly to herself. Obviously, she was making herself right at home.

I dragged myself to the stairs again. Halfway down, I stopped. This was like my worst nightmare come true. The house was a disaster area. From where I was standing I could see the marble floor of the living room, swimming with water.

Mrs T's embroidered cushion hunched at the bottom of the waterfall pool. The orchids in the glasshouse hung their heads and dripped. They'd got too much water, too suddenly. In the kitchen, I knew, the garbage disposal lay choked on a couple of metres of striped scarf, and a phone swam in Coca-Cola.

And we were locked in with all of it.

I stood motionless, my head throbbing in time with my leg.

And then I heard the front door open, and I froze. Someone was coming in!

There was a click as the door closed again, and the squeak of rubber on marble as someone in a running shoe took a quiet footstep.

Then Sunny's face peeked around the doorway.

'Sunny!' I yelled. 'Did you take the key out of the door?'

'Oh, hi, Nick,' called Sunny, looking up at me and shaking drops of water from her hair. 'Sorry I'm late. I had a tae-kwon-do class. Do you know the front lawn's just about flooded? And the path's underwater. Don't you think—?'

'Sunny! Have—you—got—the—KEY!' I roared. Was the girl deaf?

63

Sunny smiled brightly and held up the key.

'You mean this?' she said.

The relief was enormous. I slowly walked the rest of the way down the stairs, trying to get hold of myself.

By the time I reached solid ground Tom, Elmo and Liz had come crowding through the archway to the kitchen and were patting Sunny on the back.

'Right,' I said to them. 'We're out of here. We'll clean up tomorrow.'

'You'd better turn off the sprinkler,' Sunny said. 'Or the house might float away in the night.'

'Why are the sprinklers still on?' I asked Tom. 'They should have turned themselves off after thirty minutes.'

He looked guilty.

I pointed at him accusingly. 'You didn't follow the instructions!'

'I did!' he protested. 'Or at least, nearly. I just decided that since it's been dry lately, ninety minutes might be better than thirty. I thought—'

'Don't think!' I thundered. 'Go and turn it off! Now!'

Tom made a face and wandered back towards the kitchen with his hands in his pockets.

Sunny brushed at her glistening jacket. 'I'm the one who should be upset,' she said. 'I got quite wet coming in.'

'Speaking of wet, Richelle's taking her time,' Liz said, fishing for the cushion in the pool. 'What's she doing?'

'I think she's having a bath,' I said gloomily.

'Bath?' asked Sunny. 'This sounds like a fun job.'

We all just turned and glared.

'She's been ages,' Liz worried, finally pulling the cushion to the surface and putting it on the side of the pool to drip and dry out. 'I hope she's all right. She was really upset.'

'Let's go home and leave her locked in,' suggested Tom. 'It'll be the end of a perfect day for her.'

My head said 'No' but my throbbing leg kept screaming, 'Yes, yes, yes!'

Richelle appeared at the top of the stairs, dressed in a snow white bathrobe. Her hair, freshly washed and dried, fluffed around her face like a golden mist.

'Did I hear my name?' she purred.

'Richelle!' shouted Liz. 'Where'd you get that dressing-gown?'

Richelle smiled and turned around. The back of the bathrobe said GUEST in big letters across the back.

'I found it in the bathroom. Great, isn't it?' she sang. She seem to have recovered her temper completely. And the reason soon became clear.

'You should see the bathroom up here,' she went on. 'You should *see* it. Huge. Absolutely *huge*. All white. With a *huge* bath, with a whirlpool in it that works with a switch. And gold taps. And all these glass bottles of bath salts and bubble bath and shampoo and everything. It's just *heaven*!'

She sighed and shook back her hair. 'By the way, did you get the door open?' she enquired. 'And, Liz, are my clothes ready yet?'

'What's been going *on* here?' demanded Sunny.

I sighed. 'It's a long story,' I said. 'A long, sad story.'

Liz went and got Richelle's clothes, all warm from the dryer, and handed them over. Richelle smiled graciously and disappeared back upstairs to change.

'That girl's amazing,' grumbled Tom. 'Somehow she always comes out on top. *Whatever* happens, she—'

He jumped violently as the front doorbell rang.

11

Mrs Bigibbum

We all ran to the door and I peered out through the peephole. There, standing on the doorstep, was a plump, middle-aged woman holding a pot plant in her arms. I thought I recognised her but I wasn't sure. I put the chain lock across the door the way Mrs Terzis had told me to, and opened the door a crack.

The plump woman looked surprised. 'Oh, oh, hello,' she said. 'Um—Mr Terzis. Can I see him, please?'

'I'm afraid not,' I said. 'He's away.'

'Oh.' She seemed disappointed. 'Oh, I did not know.' She stood there on the doorstep looking rather helpless, clutching the plant. It was obviously some sort of orchid. I decided she must be a friend of the Terzises. Luckily the sprinklers had been turned off before. The path was still wet, but at least it wasn't streaming with water any more.

'Could I help you?' I asked. Nick Responsible Kontellis.

'Oh—oh, no.' The woman smiled nervously. 'Oh, no, it is really nothing. Just the orchid. I bring for Mr Terzis. I come back later. Or maybe—'

Suddenly I realised who she was. I took the chain off the door and swung it open a little more.

'Aren't you Mrs Vista, from the flower shop?' I asked.

She looked pleased. Her whole face came alive.

'That's right. I am Mary Vista,' she said. Suddenly we'd become old friends.

She thrust the orchid out for me to see. 'Always Mr Terzis comes to buy from me, for his wife,' she said. Her accent was quite strong, and I had to concentrate to understand her.

'Every week, he come for the flowers,' she chattered on. 'For many years, you know? Only the best, I give him. And the orchids, too. Only the best. And when this one come in, I think of him straightaway.'

The orchid flowers waved under my nose. Mrs Vista's plump face smiled expectantly behind them. Oh, I see, I thought grimly. The old girl's touting for business. Just because poor Mr T's been bashed around and lost a fortune in emeralds she's not going to do without her weekly profit boost. Well, she can think again.

I pulled the door closed a little. 'Well, Mr Terzis is away for a week,' I said firmly. 'And I'm afraid I haven't got any money. So . . .'

The woman looked shocked. 'Money? But this is a gift!' she exclaimed. 'Would I ask my best customer to pay? At this time? When he is ill, and sad? Never! No, I see it and I think, Mary, this will make Mr Terzis smile. So I put it aside.'

Her eyes widened. 'I sell it to no-one, though three people ask me. Three! I say, no! This is for Mr Terzis, my customer for ten years. So my son, he mind the shop, though his back is so bad, and I come and—'

'Oh, sorry,' I said desperately, trying to stop the flow. Boy, had I put my foot in it. I bared my teeth in a fake smile. I could feel the others fidgeting behind me.

'Hurry up!' growled Tom in my ear. 'Get on with it!'

'What's happening?' whispered another voice. A gust of perfume reached my nose. Richelle must have finally come back from playing rich ladies in the bathroom. I fleetingly wondered how many bottles she'd emptied over herself in there.

'Would you like us to take the orchid and put it in the glasshouse for Mr Terzis to find when he comes back?' Liz's voice piped up from the back.

Mrs Vista craned her neck to see where the voice had come from. Then she beamed.

'That would be very good,' she said. 'Very nice. Very good.' She pushed the orchid into my hands. I staggered a bit. The pot was heavy.

'It is *Dendrobium bigibbum phalaenopsis*,' the woman said, suddenly talking scientific names and *really* confusing me.

I heard Richelle snort with laughter. 'Bigibbum,' she hissed. Sometimes Richelle has a very childish sense of humour.

'The Cooktown orchid,' Mrs Vista explained. 'It is all on the label. You tell Mr Terzis, from Mary Vista, with many,

many good wishes.'

'I'll tell him,' I promised, and managed a more natural-looking smile. The sort that usually worked on motherly types.

She nodded happily. 'You are kind,' she said. 'You are looking after the house for Mr Terzis, yes?'

'Yes,' I said. 'I'm Nick Kontellis.'

'Ah—Demetrios Kontellis's son?' Mrs Vista's eyes brightened as she fitted me into the scheme of things. 'Of course. Mr Terzis told me about you, many times. And you and your friends help him now. You good kids.' She seemed to assume we were doing the job for free. Maybe we should be. I hadn't thought about that.

'His beautiful house,' went on Mrs Vista. 'And the orchids in bloom now. They are very beautiful, yes?'

'Yes.' I repeated. 'Hello, Cocky,' said a voice in my head.

'They are well?' she asked, as if she was talking about people.

'Would you like to see them?' I found myself saying. Sure, Mrs T had said no-one was to come into the house. But Mrs Vista wasn't any risk. She wouldn't be able to hurt a fly. Unless she bored it to death.

She held up a plump hand, shaking her head. 'Oh, no, no,' she said. 'I would not like Mr Terzis to think I push into his house. I think he might not like it.'

'He wouldn't mind,' I said. But she just looked embarrassed.

'I just sell to Mr Terzis flowers,' she said softly. 'He is a very rich, fine man. We talk, at my shop. But no more—you understand?'

I shrugged. I guess.

'Thank you,' she fluttered. 'Thank you, Nick. And now I go. Goodbye.'

We watched her as she started trotting rapidly back down the wet path. She was shaped like a pear and she wobbled as she walked.

'Bigibbum!' Richelle snorted with laughter again. 'I think they named the orchid after her. Mrs Bigibbum.'

'Don't be so mean, Richelle,' said Liz. 'Just because—'

Suddenly Mrs Vista squealed. We looked to see her staggering and waving her arms wildly. She'd lost her footing on the wet path. While we watched in horror, frozen to the spot, she struggled to get her balance back, but couldn't. She waved her arms wildly, crouched, then dropped with a squeak, flat on her bottom. Her handbag burst open and everything spilled out.

'Oh, no!' squealed Liz, as we ran out to help her.

Oh, no, I thought. Wet path. Back injury. Our fault. She could sue us.

It was at that point that I decided that Terzis Castle was cursed.

Fortunately, Mrs Vista didn't seem very badly hurt. At least she kept saying, over and over, that she was okay. But it took all of us to help her up. The back of her dress was all wet and muddy, and she groaned and gasped as we hauled her to her feet.

'Are you sure you're all right, Mrs Vista?' I asked. (Well, what else can you say at times like that?)

'Will you come in and sit down? Do you want us to ring up your son to come and get you, or anything?' Liz seemed really worried about the woman.

I just wanted to see her off the property walking on her own two feet. Sorry, but that's how it is. I cared about the Terzises. I didn't care at all about their flower lady.

Mrs Vista brushed at her dress and shook her head. 'No, no, thank you,' she murmured. 'So stupid. So sorry to cause you trouble.' She seemed very embarrassed. As you'd expect. That sort of thing makes you look a real fool. Especially if you're fat and middle-aged.

Liz looked up from the ground where, with Elmo and Sunny, she was picking up the stuff spilled from the handbag. 'No wonder you fell over, Mrs Vista,' she said soothingly. 'The path is so wet and slippery.'

Thank you, Liz, I thought. That'll be quite enough. I know you're sorry for her. But how will you feel if she sues Mr and Mrs Terzis for a fortune. Or us?

Mrs Vista took her handbag back from Liz and clutched it in her little, plump hands. 'You are kind,' she murmured. 'Good kids. Not like so many today.'

I saw Tom making a hideous face behind her back. Richelle giggled.

'Anything I can do to help you, you just call,' Mrs Vista chattered on to Liz, patting at her messed-up hair. 'Any problem with the plants, or you want some nice fresh flowers for the house, you call.' She seemed to have decided that Liz was the sensitive one around here.

'We will,' Liz promised.

'Remember that plants in a glasshouse is not like in nature,' said Mrs Vista, nodding wisely. 'A disease gets into one and pouf! Before you blink it spread and all the plants are dead. You keep careful eyes on things, kids.'

Somehow I wasn't in the mood for a botany lecture. Especially one about plants dying. I had enough troubles. Especially with Tom and Richelle mimicking Mrs Bigibbum behind her back. Any minute she could turn around and see them.

But finally the torture was over. The woman said goodbye and tottered back out through the front gate and into her car. I sighed with relief as she drove off.

'Working in a flower shop must be really good fun,' Liz said to Sunny as we walked back into the house.

Great fun, I thought. About as much fun as being dipped in acid.

Sunny nudged me in the ribs. 'Cheer up, Nick,' she said. 'Things aren't so bad.'

I didn't even reply. I guess I was feeling pretty depressed. Even a bit sorry for myself. When I look back on it I have to laugh. Because what I'd just been through at Terzis Castle was a Sunday School picnic compared with what was to come.

12

Strange signs

I was an hour late getting home. I could see that Mum was on the verge of chucking another wobbly.

'Where *were* you, Nicko?' she wailed.

'At the Terzises, Ma. You know that.'

'I try to ring you. Nothing happen.'

'I was probably on the phone,' I said.

'You? No, Nicko, you wouldn't ring up on the Terzis phone.'

'No, you're right. It probably wasn't me. What's for dinner?'

While she was cooking dinner I told her about Mrs Vista and the orchid. I drew a veil over Mrs Bigibbum's exciting exit.

'Mary Vista is a *lovely* lady,' Mum said. Everyone to her is a *lovely* lady—if they're not a *lovely* man.

'Hey!' Dad yelled out from the living room. 'Come quick!'

We ran, but not fast enough. The news item he'd been watching was over.

'They found out about the man who robbed Stephanos,' he said. 'His name was Roach or Rouse or something. He worked at the pub in Mint Beach. They think someone meet him there, get him to do the job. Hired thug.'

'Any word on the guy who was driving the car?' *Or the emeralds?* Somehow I couldn't put the thought into words.

'No,' my father said heavily. 'Nothing.'

After dinner I called the phone company, in secret, to report the dead phone. I arranged for the guy to come while we were at Terzis Castle the next day. Then I did some homework. Then I mucked around with *Escape from Zargos* again, got nowhere, and started thinking about the driver of the getaway car.

I'd seen him, from a distance. But I couldn't picture him. I shut my eyes. In my mind there was just this shape sitting at the wheel. It was so bright on the other side of the car that all I could see was his silhouette.

Suddenly my eyes flew open. I stood up and started pacing. I'd thought of something. There was something about the guy's head. It was kind of flat. It didn't bulge out in the back as much as heads usually do. Or was that just something about the way he wore his hair?

Was this a real memory or was I imagining what I'd seen? Maybe I was. Maybe I wasn't. Should I tell the police?

I decided to let the idea simmer for a while before I rushed into anything. I didn't want to make a fool of myself.

Wednesday at Terzis Castle wasn't as bad as Tuesday, but it came close.

The six of us had spent about an hour actually working at the Castle the day before. Six Teen Power hours. And what did we have to show for it? A broken telephone system, a bunged-up garbage disposal, and a big mess to clean up. I wasn't too happy as I walked through the gate.

Richelle, Sunny, Liz and Elmo were waiting at the door. I was very pleased to see that Tom wasn't. Then, just as I was about to put the key in the door he jumped out of the bushes.

'Boo!' he yelled.

By the time I'd scraped my heart off the roof of my mouth I realised that they were all doubled over, screaming with laughter.

'Very funny,' I said coldly. 'Tell me when it's okay to stop laughing.'

'You forgot to check the bushes, Nick,' Tom giggled. 'Naughty, naughty.'

'I saw you in there, Tom,' I lied.

'Don't forget to take the key out of the lock,' he said.

'Thanks, Tom,' I said. 'I'll try to remember.'

I got the burglar alarm code right straightaway. So far, so good. I put the key into the lock on the inside of the door. So farther, so better.

I got Sunny and Tom started on cleaning the marble floor. A lot of the water from yesterday had dried up but there were puddles here and there, especially around the pool, and stains and streaks everywhere. Elmo went to feed the birds.

Liz went back to dusting. Richelle wandered to the glasshouse. I went to the kitchen, to feed the fish and check out the phone and the garbage disposal.

The phone was still dead. I looked at my watch. The phone guy should arrive soon. At least that problem would be solved. I wondered how much it would cost.

I fed the fish. They looked all right, anyway. At least none of them was floating on the surface yet. But I had a feeling, the way we were going, that it was only a matter of time.

Then I tackled the garbage disposal. I cut Tom's scarf off right down at the plughole with a pair of kitchen scissors, then turned the taps on full and pushed the button, crossing my fingers.

There was a roaring, straining motor sound and then, suddenly, something more encouraging. A busy sort of whirr I recognised. The last bits of wool disappeared down the hole. It looked like all was well. Thank heavens for that.

I dumped the scarf end into the rubbish bin under the sink, and blinked. There were our Coke cans from yesterday. And tucked down beside them the torn wrapper from a pack of chocolate-chip cookies. I picked it up. Tom, I thought furiously. He opened biscuits and pigged the lot while he was in the kitchen yesterday, and thought he'd get away with it.

On an impulse I pulled open the refrigerator door. More signs of Tom's jaws on the loose. A half packet of cheese left open and drying out. A chewed-looking piece of peperoni. A big hole where the last of the Coke cans had been.

'Nick!' Richelle's voice interrupted my angry thoughts. I looked up and saw her standing near the fish tank.

'What's up?'

'One of the orchids looks sick. Really sick.'

'Is it Mrs Bigibbum's Cooktown orchid?' I asked wearily. I wasn't surprised to hear about the orchid. Somehow I'd come to expect disaster in this house.

'No, this is a different one. Come and see.'

I hurried towards her, tripped over the step between the kitchen and dining room areas and nearly fell into the fish tank for the second time in two days.

'Are you all right?' she asked. 'Your eyes look weird. And why are you falling over your own feet? That's Tom's job.'

'The step,' I mumbled. 'It's in a stupid place.'

She raised her eyebrows and led the way into the living room.

The orchid she showed me was sick all right. Its leaves were drooping down over the sides of its pot, and the flowers were limp and rubbery.

'It probably got too much water yesterday. When you soaked me,' Richelle said nastily. 'We'd better get rid of it before the Terzises come home.'

'Are you kidding?' I said. 'They know every plant in the house.'

'Well, we'd better do something. If this thing's got a disease it could spread to the other orchids, like Mrs Bigibbum said.'

I put my face in my hands.

'What's wrong now?' asked Liz, coming into the glasshouse. She hunched her shoulders and wrinkled her nose. 'It's hot in here,' she complained. 'Hot and steamy. And something smells funny.'

I showed her the sick orchid. 'I think it's this,' I said. 'It's got orchid fever or orchid spotted spitting virus or something.'

'We'd better take it to Mrs Vista,' said Liz. 'Maybe she could cure it.'

A tiny flame of hope began flickering in my chest. 'Do you think?'

'Worth a try,' said Liz. She took the orchid from me and carried it to the front door so we wouldn't forget to take it when we left.

'Someone's got mud on their shoes,' she said when she came back. She pointed at a brown smear on one of the white living room rugs.

'Tom!'

He was the obvious suspect. He must have got mud on his shoes when he was hiding in the bushes. He denied it of course. Just as he denied eating the chocolate chip cookies, the cheese and the peperoni. But I knew that didn't mean a thing, and I told him so.

'Get off my back, Kontellis!' He went all pink and sulked like a little kid.

There was something about Tom. Something about the bands on his teeth, the long, skinny arms and legs, the silly clothes, the grey-blue eyes, the messy hair—something about him that screamed: 'Kill! Kill! Kill!'

Well, that's what it screamed at me. I just wanted to strangle him and know I'd got away with it.

Resisting the urge, I stormed off. In the laundry cupboard was a spray can of something called Carpet Prim. 'The last word in carpet cleaning,' according to the label.

It said it was for those hard-to-shift carpet stains. All you had to do was to spray it on and wait. I went out to the living room and sprayed it on the mud and then waited. And waited. And waited. While nothing happened.

When I brushed it away, the stain was still staring me in the face, thumbing its nose and daring me to try one last remedy.

I threw down the can and said my own last word in carpet cleaning—which I can't repeat.

Mrs T would have a stroke if she saw her beautiful living room now, I thought. Water and dirty streaks everywhere. Mud on one of her rugs. Her embroidered cushion sodden and wrinkly. One of her orchids dying by the front door.

All I need now, I thought, scrubbing away at the stain that seemed to be getting worse instead of better the longer I worked on it, all I need now is for her to come home unexpectedly. Or for someone who knows her to come. That'd be the finish.

I should have known better than to let the idea cross my mind. Because, of course, straightaway the doorbell rang.

13

Darkness and light

It's the phone guy, I thought to myself. It must be. It has to be.

It wasn't. It was Miles Silvestro.

I'd met him before, at a couple of the Terzis's parties. Mum and Mrs T were always saying how patient and wonderful he was.

Mr T wasn't so enthusiastic. Miles was useful to him, I think, because he was the kind of prissy fusspot who'd do all the boring business stuff Mr T didn't want to do himself. But Mr T didn't really like him.

Neither did I. In fact, I'd always thought he was a real pain—and I think he felt much the same about me.

He rang the bell again.

I tossed around the choices I had. If I didn't open the door, he'd tell the Terzises that Teen Power Inc. hadn't been at the house when they were supposed to be. If I *did* open the door, he'd come in and see the mess, and tell the Terzises all about *that*.

Either way, he'd win and I'd lose.

I made my decision. I put the security chain on and opened the door a crack.

'Yes?' I asked, then acted surprised. 'Oh, hi, Mr Silvestro.'

'Ah, Nick. I thought I'd drop by to make sure everything was all right,' Miles Silvestro said, leaning forward and peering suspiciously at me. He was so close I could smell the peppermint on his breath, and see the dandruff on his shoulders.

'Oh, it is,' I said. 'Everything's absolutely fine.'

'I tried to call you. The phone seems to be out of order,' he said, pushing at the door. The chain caught it and kept it from continuing on its way through the side of my head. 'Nick, dear boy, let me in.'

Not by the hair of my chinny-chin-chin. 'I'm really sorry, Mr Silvestro,' I burbled, trying to look young and embarrassed. 'But Mr Terzis said we weren't allowed to let anyone into the house. Anyone at all.'

He pressed his lips together and squinted. I hadn't seen a more furious look since—well, since the day before when I half-drowned Richelle. Then he forced a smile. Believe me, the angry look was more appealing.

'Mr Terzis didn't mean *me*, Nick,' he said. He rattled the door against the chain. 'Come on. Don't be ridiculous.'

I shook my head. 'I don't dare,' I whispered. 'Mr Terzis definitely said—'

Silvestro's nostrils flared into little circles.

'Nick,' he said softly. 'As you very well know, I am in charge of things in Mr Terzis's absence. I handle all his affairs when he goes away—and that includes matters regarding his home. Now please let me in! Or I'll think you have something to hide.'

How could he think such a thing?

Tom and Sunny had come up beside me by now, and the three of us stood looking out through the crack.

Silvestro's little eyes just kept darting from one face to another.

'I've had enough of this,' he exclaimed. 'I've never heard of such a thing. Open the door!'

'I'm sorry. But I can't,' I said very slowly so that he'd get the message.

A white line appeared around his mouth. Bright red patches appeared on both his cheeks. I hoped he wouldn't have some sort of attack.

'You are a very stupid boy,' he hissed. 'You haven't heard the last of this.'

He turned and walked rapidly back down the path. I watched him go. Well, I'd done my best.

We all worked like dogs for an hour after that. Most of the time was spent fixing up things that had happened since we arrived, including fingermarks on walls upstairs that everyone denied were theirs, another stain discovered on the stair carpet, and an attempted revival of the embroidered cushion. We also had to put more water into the waterfall pool.

No-one else came to the door except two guys in suits selling their church. I told them we weren't interested. They blessed me anyway.

Finally, all the routine jobs were done and the house was looking better. There hadn't been any more disasters, except that when I went to check the upstairs phones I discovered the workroom door had locked itself. I must have set the lock by mistake when I went to check the phone before. So there'd be no dusting in the workroom till the Terzises came back. Another black mark for Teen Power Inc.

Then Tom and I discovered we'd both fed the fish. Well, all we could do was hope they didn't overeat and die. I told Tom that if they did it would be his fault. He shouldn't have just gone ahead and fed them without asking me first. He said he'd had no idea things could die if they overate. I told him he was lucky it didn't happen to humans. Not overnight, anyway.

We set the alarm and let ourselves out of the house. Sunny, Tom, Richelle and Elmo went home. Liz and I, with the sick orchid, headed off towards Mrs Bigibbum's flower shop. And only when we were halfway there did I remember that the phone guy had never turned up.

Mrs Vista frowned at the drooping orchid. She shook her head. 'Have you been careful watering, kids? Too much water as bad as too little, you know.'

'Oh, I know,' I said, looking innocent.

'Has it been fed too much, maybe? This too can—'

'I don't know,' I broke in. 'Mrs Terzis didn't say anything about feeding.'

'It seems to smell funny,' Liz put in.

'Funny?' repeated Mrs Vista. She put her nose close to the pot and sniffed deeply. 'Rot!' she pronounced.

I thought she was saying Liz was talking rot, but it turned out she meant that the plant was on its way out because its bulb was going rotten, or something.

'I think this one is finished,' she pronounced sadly. 'I give you another one just like it. Wait!' Before I could say anything she'd taken the sad orchid away and disappeared into a back room.

I looked around at all the flowers. The shop was stacked with them.

'Aren't they gorgeous?' sighed Liz, waving her arm around.

'Flowers all together remind me of funerals,' I said. 'This place is an undertaker's fantasy minus the corpse.'

'Oh, *Nick*!'

After a few minutes, Mrs Vista came puffing back into the room with another orchid in her arms. It was strong and healthy, but otherwise looked so like the dying one that I wondered for a minute if she'd performed some lightning cure on it.

This cheered me up a lot. With a bit of luck I wouldn't even have to tell the Terzises what had happened. Even if the new orchid cost me everything I was making out of the job, it would be worth it.

'I can't pay for it now, Mrs Vista,' I mumbled. 'Would it be all right if I—'

She flapped her hands. 'Don't worry,' she beamed. 'No charge. My pleasure, kids.'

Liz thanked her from the bottom of her heart. I thanked her from the bottom of my wallet. So we were both very sincere.

She put her finger to her lips. 'It our little secret, kids,' she said. 'But no more you overwater.' She looked a little shy and pulled out a card from her apron pocket. 'I make you a note. For reminding you. You put on glasshouse door, remind all your friends. Promise?' She handed the card to Liz who read it quickly, smiled and nodded.

'Okay,' I said. 'And thanks again, Mrs Vista.'

I really did feel grateful to the old bat. She might be annoying, but at least she knew her stuff. I only wished we had a tame pet-shop owner who'd give me free tropical fish when the time came.

At the door, Mrs Vista put her hand up next to her nose and gave me one of those little finger waves.

'Bysie-bye,' she called.

'Bysie-bye,' Liz and I called back.

Good grief.

'Where were you?' Mum demanded when I got home. 'And, Nicko, why you bring an orchid home?'

Interrogation time at Kontellis Castle.

'I'm looking after it,' I said. Best, I thought, to keep it simple.

'Stephanos love his orchids,' said Mum doubtfully. 'He wouldn't like anything to happen.'

'Exactly.'

'Is that you, Nicko?' Dad called out from the other room.

'Yes, Dad.'

'That Miles Silvestro call you.'

'What did he want?'

'He don't say. He want you to ring him back. He don't sound too happy. Were you rude to him?'

'Rude? Me?'

'Anyway he say he just want to have a talk. *Chat*, he say.'

The thought of chatting with Miles Silvestro was about as appealing as having my fingernails pulled out by terrorists. I decided to give it a miss.

'I've got a lot of homework,' I said. 'I'll ring him tomorrow.'

14

Toil and trouble

Thursday.

I could feel it building up all day. This nervy, angry feeling. I just kept thinking more and more about the Castle: the water everywhere, the dead phone, the work. Somehow it was like running in soft sand: two steps forward and one step back. I wished I'd never heard of the job, let alone volunteered for it.

After school I raced home to get the orchid, then staggered along with it to Terzis Castle. Mum would have driven me, but I couldn't risk her wanting to look inside the house. She'd find out about the phone, for a start.

When I got there the others were waiting for me, sitting talking in a circle on the front lawn. They looked at me silently. I was sure they'd been talking about me. We were supposed to be going to a movie together after work. Already I was thinking of excuses not to go.

I took a breath, sauntered down the path, and raised an eyebrow at them. None of them moved. I opened the door and turned off the burglar alarm, remaining cool as a cucumber—well, on the outside, anyway.

'Anybody out there want to earn some money?' I asked super-politely.

'Aww, do we have to?' Tom asked.

'Not if you don't want to, Tom,' I said. 'Nobody's going to make you do anything. You can sit there and frighten the birds away for all I care.'

They all gave each other a what's-eating-him look and then got up and came into the Castle.

I took the orchid into the glasshouse and put it down with relief. Then I frowned as I saw what Liz was doing. She was actually sticking Mrs Vista's note to the door. The others crowded around to read it, giggling.

'Liz, what are you doing?' I demanded.

'I promised Mrs Vista, Nick.'

'That's ridiculous, Liz. She'll never know.'

'*I'll* know,' Liz said haughtily. I could have shaken her.

Tom read the notice out loud in a fairly good imitation of Mrs Vista's voice.

'Careful! Don't overwater. Leave damp without flooding them. Don't use the orchid food again. Water when plants ready. Remember, I'll help. Keep happy kids, and busy. Then while working you won't get stressed out.'

Everyone screamed with laughter, except Liz and me.

Don't get stressed out. Yuck. It sounded like it had been written by Little Bo Peep on a bad day. But still, I didn't like them laughing.

'Keep happy, kids, and busy,' screeched Richelle. 'How old does she think we are, six? That Mrs Bigibbum is a real drop kick.'

'Don't call her that,' I muttered. 'Her name's Vista.'

She stared at me.

'Just check the plants, Richelle, and then water them, if that wouldn't be too much trouble,' I said.

'What should I check them for, Nickers?'

'Spots.'

'What kind of spots?'

'Any kind of spots,' I said. 'And limp leaves and . . . anything! Just look at the things and see if they're all about to croak, okay? Oh, forget it.'

'Touchy, aren't we?'

'Speak for yourself,' I mumbled.

I pushed my way past her. I saw something glinting in the waterfall pool and bent to fish it out. A crumpled drink can.

'Civilised people live here, Tom,' I said, pointing at it. 'Could you just get it into your thick head that we're here to clean up, not make more mess?'

'That's not mine,' said Tom immediately. Of course.

'No, it wouldn't be,' I snapped. I slapped my forehead. 'Stupid of me. I keep forgetting about the poltergeist.'

They just looked at me. I clenched my fists.

'If anybody wants me I'll be in the kitchen,' I said.

Richelle flicked her hair back.

'Who would want you?'

In the kitchen I could hear them moving around, the odd clunk and bang. Sunny laughing. Tom laughing. I tried the phone. Nothing. I looked at the fish. They looked back. How do you tell if a fish is feeling well? I wished the phone guy would come. Why don't these people come when they say they will?

Back in the living room there was no-one in sight. Where were they, watching TV? Maybe they'd discovered the swimming pool. I was about to call out when a voice yelled.

'Yoo-hoo.'

I looked up to see the whole gang sitting on limbs of the tree.

'What are you doing?!' I demanded.

'We're on strike,' Richelle said.

'What are you talking about? Get down from there before you break the tree!'

'Not till you get civilised.'

'Me?' I asked.

'You!' they all said together.

That was it. That was the final straw.

'Get out of here, all of you!' I screamed. 'Get down out of that tree and get out of this house!'

'Nick—' Liz began.

'Never mind! I don't want to hear it. Just climb down and get out!'

I watched as they started to climb silently down, lowering themselves to the rocks in the pond and then hopping to dry land. I could feel myself calming down now but I was still panting like I'd run the one-hundred-metre dash. I walked quickly to the front door. They followed.

'I don't know what's wrong with you, Nick,' said Liz, as I swung the door open.

I pressed my lips together. 'You don't seem to understand that—that—' I couldn't go on. I couldn't explain how bad I felt.

'What?' Sunny asked. 'What?'

I took a breath. 'How would you like it if somebody stole a million dollars worth of emeralds that weren't insured from you?' I burst out. 'When you've worked so hard to build up a business? All your life?'

Suddenly the dammed-up words were rushing out. Now I couldn't stop them. 'When you've always been generous, and friendly, and liked everyone, so that even old ladies who run flower shops will do anything for you? For free? Then a bunch of kids you're actually *paying* to help you, start mucking around in your house, treating it like some fairground, gutsing all your food, messing it up—'

'Nick, there were a couple of accidents,' said Liz quietly. 'The house is fine. I don't know how the marks on the walls got there, but we've cleaned them off . . .'

'I haven't eaten much food,' Tom put in. 'And I didn't put mud on the rug.'

I turned away from him.

'Who did, then?' I muttered.

They filed out through the door and onto the grass. Liz hung back. She put her hand on my arm. 'Nick, the emeralds might still be found,' she said gently. Now she'd taken in why I was so upset she'd switched from being angry with me to being sorry for me.

I shook my head. 'They'll never be found now. It's been too long. Nearly a week. It's hopeless. It was probably hopeless the moment they left this house.'

Richelle was looking at me with her head on one side. 'What makes you so sure they did?' she asked.

'What are you talking about?' I asked.

'Never mind.'

'No, what did you say?'

'I was just thinking, maybe the guy in the mask didn't take the emeralds after all,' Richelle said.

'*What?*'

'Maybe he didn't have them with him when he left the house,' she went on, slowly, so poor, stupid me could follow her.

If it was anyone else I would have thought they were kidding, but Richelle didn't make jokes like this.

'He went right *past* us,' jeered Sunny.

'I know. That's what just made me think of it,' Richelle said. 'He was right where Nick and Liz are now and we were right here.' She pointed to the ground.

'So?'

'So I don't think he had the emeralds with him. He couldn't have.'

93

'How do you know that?' Liz asked.

'Well, one of his hands had a knife in it and the other one was open. He was waving at us with an open hand, remember?'

'He'd have had the emeralds in his pocket, dummy,' said Tom. Richelle smirked one of those special Richelle smirks.

'Pockets?' she said. 'Pockets in an *Alezis d'Alpine* tracksuit? Where have you been?'

My heart thudded. 'Are you saying that *Alezis d'Alpine* tracksuits don't have pockets?'

'Not unless they've changed them.'

'Are you *sure*?' I asked.

'*Absolutely* sure,' she said.

Liz's hand tightened on my arm. 'They must still be in the house, then,' she whispered. 'And when you think about it—'

I knew what she was going to say. I could hear Mr T's voice in my head, too. Talking to the cops. Telling the story. The man in the mask took the emeralds in his hand. He ran from the workroom, with Mr T after him. He ran all over the first floor, then downstairs. He fell over, twice. He was an amateur. He was panicking.

'He could have dropped them,' Elmo said slowly. 'Anywhere. They could be anywhere.' He was getting excited.

Richelle nodded, smiling, and began checking out her fingernails.

'Treasure hunt!' hooted Tom. He nudged Sunny, his eyes gleaming. 'Let's go!' They both grinned at me.

I felt myself grinning back. And, for once, being glad that Tom was like he was. In fact, glad they were all like they were. Suddenly we were all on the same side again.

15

Green for danger

We went back into the house, shut the door and locked it. Liz put the key in her pocket. 'Just to be on the safe side,' she said. 'You never know.'

I could see that she'd slipped into detective mode and was playing the part to the full. From now on, with Liz, there'd be possible enemies lurking everywhere. Even in a locked house with only her friends in it.

'Would the guy have hidden them somewhere?' Elmo said. 'Maybe when he was running away he put them in a drawer or something, thinking he'd go back later.'

'No!' Liz shook her head. 'He was panicking. He'd have just kept running. If he dropped them, it was by accident.'

'All right,' said Sunny, jiggling up and down on the spot, busting to get moving. 'But *where* did he drop them?'

'I know!' yelled Tom, his eyes popping. 'I know!' He made a dash for the stairs.

Elmo went to check the birdhouse. Liz went into the glasshouse. 'What better place for stones to be than in a flowerpot?' she said. I didn't like her chances. From what Mr T had said, the robber didn't go into the glasshouse.

Richelle and Sunny followed Tom upstairs. They'd remembered that the upstairs rooms hadn't been cleaned. As far as they were concerned, that was the place to look. Behind doors, under furniture, in that maze of bedrooms, bathrooms and little sitting rooms.

I stayed with the most obvious possibility—the waterfall pool. A little plastic bag of stones could lie there among the weeds and rocks for years without being noticed. And, after all, Mr T and the man in the mask had fallen down the stairs just here.

Suddenly I heard Tom's voice.

'I've found them!' he yelled. 'I've found the emeralds!'

'Tom!' squeaked Liz, pelting out of the glasshouse. 'Where were they?'

I looked up to see Tom standing at the head of the stairs. He held out a clenched fist. There was a slight smile on his face.

'They were in Richelle's bathroom,' he called. 'Boy, did Richelle leave a mess there, too. You should speak to her about that, Nick.'

'I did *not* leave a mess,' said Richelle, appearing beside him, frowning. 'I was very careful not to.'

'The emeralds!' I yelled. 'Tom! Show me!'

He grinned and chucked something down to me. Something that glinted green as it flew through the air.

I grabbed it. But even before I opened my hand to look at

the green throat lozenges in their clear plastic packet, I knew I'd been had.

'Great work, Tom,' I said. 'Great work.'

I stuffed the packet into my pocket and went back to the pool. I didn't want him to see just how disappointed I was. He'd really had me going for a minute.

I searched every millimetre of that pool. Except for the crumpled can I'd seen there earlier, there was nothing in it but rocks and weed. As I fished the can out I saw Elmo go upstairs to join the others. He shrugged at me. He'd obviously drawn a blank in the birdhouse.

I stood up, arching my cramped back. Liz came out of the glasshouse. She shook her head. 'Nothing,' she said mournfully.

I hadn't thought she'd find anything there. Still, she'd really wanted to try it. And there were lots of places in a glasshouse where five little pebbles in a tiny plastic bag could lie unnoticed. Fair enough.

'Where's everybody else?' she asked.

'They're all upstairs somewhere,' I said.

She looked up. 'It's awfully quiet,' she commented.

I shrugged. 'Hey, up there!' I yelled. 'Where are you?'

No answer. Game time again, I thought.

'I'll go and find them,' Liz said. 'Help them look. I suppose it is more likely the guy dropped the stones up there.'

I shook the water from the crumpled can. 'This is stupid, you know, Liz,' I muttered. 'If the emeralds were here we'd have found them by now. Richelle's probably wrong about that guy's tracksuit not having pockets.'

'I don't think she would be,' Liz said. 'If there's one thing Richelle knows, it's clothes.'

I couldn't argue with that, but I watched her climbing the stairs without much hope. She turned into one of the corridors, calling, and disappeared from view.

I waited for a minute, then yelled to her. But she didn't answer. I yelled again. There was only silence. I couldn't believe it. Even Liz was still willing to mess me around.

I walked through the archway into the dining room, and on into the kitchen to throw the can away. With every step I grew more depressed, and more irritated.

I'll just go and leave them to it, I thought angrily. It was a kid's idea, and I couldn't do it anyway, I realised. Liz had the key. I couldn't get out without it.

The silence was thick. I fiddled with the can in my hand. Uncrumpled it. Looked at it.

It was a beer can.

But Tom didn't drink beer.

I went to the fridge and opened it. There were a few other cans of beer there, just like the one I was holding.

The can hadn't been in the pool when we arrived.

But Tom didn't drink beer. None of us drank beer.

I turned away from the fridge. The kitchen stretched gleaming around me. I'd stood just here nearly a week ago, when I came to get ice for Mr Terzis. Then the marble floor had been puddled with water. Slippery. And there'd been blood.

Suddenly I shivered. I began to walk back to the living room. My feet made hardly any sound on the marble floor. The fish cruised in their tank. Orange, black, white, red, bright blue. Clean bubbling water, clean green weed, clean pebbly bottom, clean hard glass. They were trapped, in a clean, luxurious, silent world. Like me.

Trapped. I tried to get rid of the feeling. My hands were starting to sweat. I reached the living room and made myself walk to the foot of the stairs.

'Hey!' I yelled, as loudly as I could. 'Hey! Stop fooling round!'

No answer.

The orchids bloomed, behind glass. Trapped. There was a single squawk from a parrot in the birdhouse. Trapped.

I looked up at the tree, rising high to the glass dome. For the first time the idea of a dead tree in the middle of a house seemed more weird than wonderful.

A dead tree. Who would want a dead tree in the middle of their house?

Liz was right. I suddenly knew what she meant about the house being like a tomb. It was about as cosy as a slab in the local morgue. Terzis Crypt.

My eye fell on Mrs Vista's notice, still taped to the glasshouse door. I was glad Liz had put it there now. It was something silly and human in the middle of all this cold perfection.

CAREFUL! DON'T OVERWATER. LEAVE DAMP WITHOUT FLOODING THEM. DON'T USE THE ORCHID FOOD AGAIN. WATER WHEN PLANTS READY. REMEMBER I'LL HELP. KEEP HAPPY KIDS, AND BUSY. THEN WHILE WORKING YOU WON'T GET STRESSED OUT.

Mrs Vista wasn't perfect. But she was warm, and willing to help. So even if she did write wet messages that barely made sense . . . I looked again at the note and shook my head. It was certainly funny, the way she put things.

I concentrated on the note. It helped me screen out other thoughts. The silence was pressing on my ears. The carefully printed words blurred in front of my eyes.

Then, as though someone had pressed a button, a thousand light bulbs switched on in my head.

My mind was suddenly filled with pictures. Clear and bright. The little hero in *Escape from Zargos*. Tom's face as he argued with me about the cheese, the peperoni, the chocolate chip cookies. The crumpled can in the pool. The stained rug that no-one had muddied. The dirty marks on the walls that no-one had touched. Richelle at the top of the stairs, saying she hadn't left the bathroom in a mess.

If she hadn't, who had? If Tom hadn't eaten that food, who had? If no-one in Teen Power Inc. put mud on the floor, who had? If we hadn't drunk the beer, who had?

Someone else.

Now the lights were on, I couldn't turn them off again. I could clearly see the facts now. I had to face them.

Someone else was in the house. Someone had been living here secretly for days. Eating food from the fridge, using the bathroom, hiding during our visits so we wouldn't suspect, leaving traces I'd been too stupid to understand. Till now.

Why?

Logic supplied the answer. The emeralds. Someone had been doing for days what we had just begun doing this afternoon. Searching for the emeralds.

Who?

The driver of the getaway car. The man who probably organised the whole robbery. The only person who knew that the emeralds hadn't left the house.

The man in the mask had fallen into the car, unable to speak, and then he was killed in the crash. But the emeralds weren't on him. The driver would have heard on the news that Mr Terzis *thought* the emeralds were gone. So then he'd have realised that they must have been dropped or hidden somewhere in the house.

He'd come back to find them. He was here. Somewhere.

102

And he'd probably been listening to us. My heart nearly stopped beating. He'd have known we were searching for the emeralds. He'd have heard Tom shout that he'd found them.

He probably had the others.

I ran on my toes to the front door. The phone was dead. But the burglar alarm wasn't. I pushed the button. Nothing happened. I pushed it again. Nothing.

Then I realised what had happened. I'd thought it was strange that the workroom was locked. The guy was there. That's where he'd been hiding from us all this time. And now he'd turned off the alarm at the master switch.

No phone. No alarm. No way out.

16

Rescue

I'm no hero. Movies and computer games are one thing. But I know that in real life heroes are as likely to end up dead as riding off into the sunset.

But in this case, what else could I do except climb those stairs?

I thought of just lying low. Waiting, hoping that someone would come. The phone repair guy, maybe. Or Mrs Vista. Or Miles Silvestro. Or even those guys wanting to talk to us about their church. I wished now that I'd been nicer to them.

But I couldn't just wait. For a start, no-one might come at all. And the guy could be torturing the others up there in the workroom. He could be killing them. He could be doing anything.

I couldn't go barehanded. I went to the kitchen and got this spiked hammer that the Terzises used for flattening steak. No way I'd take a knife. No way I'd take the guy a weapon like that. What I was planning was dangerous enough anyway.

Back in the living room, I stood at the bottom of the

stairs, trying to stop my hands from shaking.

I started up the stairs. At least marble didn't creak. I found I was panting. I was so scared I thought I'd faint. I couldn't believe I was doing this.

I got to the top of the stairs. I began creeping down one of the corridors, along the thick carpet. The panting had stopped now. Now I had to keep reminding myself to breathe.

Then the back of my neck started to prickle. I stopped. Suddenly I knew that I wasn't alone. I don't know if I'd actually heard the scuff of a foot on the floor behind me or if it was just that some sixth sense warned me. All I knew was there was someone lurking there, behind me, waiting their chance to—

Before I could blink, or move a muscle, a powerful hand clamped over my mouth and pulled me backwards into a bedroom. I tried to yell but it was no use. The hand on my mouth was too tight and the other arm was crushing my windpipe.

In a second I was on the floor. The hand was still covering my mouth, smothering any sound.

It was then that I saw her face.

'Don't talk, Nick!' Sunny whispered. 'This is no joke. Keep your mouth shut or we're both dead!'

Slowly she took her hand from my mouth.

'There's someone here,' she whispered.

'I know,' I panted. 'In the workroom.'

She raised her eyebrows in surprise, but typically she didn't waste time asking how I knew.

'He's got all the others,' she said. 'He must have grabbed them one by one. I didn't know what was happening at first. I just couldn't find anyone. Then I actually saw him get Liz. It was just pure luck that he didn't see me. And I saw the others in the room. Tied up. Gagged. He wants the emeralds.'

'I know,' I said again.

'He seems to think we have them,' Sunny whispered. 'Why would he think that?'

'When Tom yelled out that he'd found them, he must have heard, and believed it. I told Tom his sense of humour would get him killed one day.'

Sunny nodded. But she wasn't really listening. She bent to tighten the laces on her gym shoes.

'Okay,' she muttered. 'Now. I don't think he knows exactly how many of us there are. All he knows is that someone was still downstairs while he was catching people upstairs. He's not too clever, I don't think. But he's dangerous. He wants those emeralds. He's getting desperate.'

'So what do we do?' I honestly had no idea.

'We can't get out and go for help because Liz has the key to the front door,' said Sunny. 'And the guy's got Liz. So—here's the plan. Just do as I say and don't think about it too much, okay?'

I listened, swallowed, nodded, feeling myself sweat while her voice went on, calmly outlining her idea. That girl has nerves of steel, I thought. Wish I did. My lip started twitching. I concentrated on holding it still. I couldn't let her see how bad I felt.

'Just take deep breaths, Nick,' said Sunny, glancing at me. 'This plan takes two of us. I need you.'

Guess she wasn't fooled.

❁

Sunny went down the stairs very quietly indeed. But when she clambered up to the first floor again, a minute later, she was shouting.

'Hey, you guys, come out!' she yelled. 'This is no time for jokes. I've got the emeralds!'

She stood silent for a moment, waiting at the head of the stairs. 'Don't be silly!' she shouted again. 'Listen, are you coming out, or not? Because I'm taking these to the police. On my own if I have to!'

She folded her arms and turned to look out over the living room area, so that her back faced the doorways and corridors. She tapped her foot. 'This is your last chance!' she warned. 'In thirty seconds I'm leaving.'

She didn't pay any attention to me, watching from behind a half-open door. She didn't seem to hear someone else's feet brushing the carpet as he moved rapidly towards her. She didn't seem to sense that she was being hunted. She looked at her watch and sighed impatiently.

I bit my knuckles as a man I'd never seen before moved into my eye line. He was crouching slightly as he moved along. He turned slightly and I saw that head, that flatness at the back. It was the driver of the getaway car!

His hands were stretching out towards the back of Sunny's neck.

Sunny, look out! He's right behind you! The words trembled on my tongue. But I bit them back. I knew I couldn't call out. I just had to wait there, powerless, watching. I had to trust her.

The crouching figure sprang, and at exactly the same moment Sunny lashed backwards with a foot, kicking him in the leg. Tae-kwon-do is supposed to be used only for defence, she always says. I hope I'm not around if they ever change the rules.

The man reeled backwards, staggering, doubling up.

Sunny, without a word, flung herself onto the banister and slid down.

'You little . . .'

Half-limping half-running, jumping from step to step, the man plunged after her.

'I'll get you!' he yelled. 'And when I do—!'

'You'll have to catch me first!' Sunny yelled back.

There was a splash now, and a thump, and then another splash. But I wasn't watching any more. I was following my orders. Racing for the workroom.

There, huddled on the floor, were Elmo, Liz, Tom and Richelle, all tied up and gagged with heavy plastic packing tape. Elmo's eyes stared up at me, pleading to be released, his mouth wide open, the tape wound around and around pinning his jaw against his neck. From the panic in his eyes I knew that he was suffocating, that he wasn't getting enough air through his nose to keep him conscious much longer.

I rushed for the master switch to the burglar alarm, switched it on, and pushed the button that would signal trouble to the cops. I knew that was the first, the most important thing to do. Then I made for Elmo. I grabbed the end of the tape and whipped it around and around his head.

'Quiet!' I whispered. 'Not a word!'

When I had the tape off his mouth, I untaped his hands and then released the others.

Elmo lay gasping on the floor, struggling to catch his breath again.

'Where is he?' Liz whispered.

'Sunny's handling him. Just do as I say: run for the stairs. Don't try anything! Just get out of the house, understand? Liz, remember you've got the key. The police are on their way.'

I led them, running, through the maze of corridors to the top of the stairs. Sunny was now halfway up the tree. She held her clenched fist in the air. 'I've got the emeralds,' she was calling to the man in the pool below. 'You'll never get them! May as well give up!'

The man was roaring with rage. He started heaving himself up into the tree, slipping on the shiny, varnished surface, reaching for Sunny's feet.

'Sunny!' cried Liz in terror.

17

Hostage

I pulled at Liz's arm and made her run with us down the stairs.

The man twisted his neck and saw us. An expression of baffled rage crossed his face.

'Go! Get out!' Sunny yelled to us, kicking at the man's grasping hands.

I still had the meat mallet in my hand. Not an excellent weapon for a hero, maybe. But not a bad missile for a kid in an emergency.

I threw it. It spun through the air, connecting beautifully with the back of the man's head. He jerked. His hold on the tree loosened. Sunny's foot connected with his shoulder—and he was falling.

We raced for the front door. There was a huge splash behind us as the man hit the water. I looked back to see Sunny leaping for the stairs from her tree like a glider possum. She swung herself over the banister and pounded down after us.

When she reached us Liz was still wrestling with the key in the door. We could hear the man groaning, struggling up and out of the pool.

'Hurry!' shrieked Richelle.

The key turned. The door swung open. We shot outside like bullets from a gun.

And there, toddling down the path, was Mrs Vista, another orchid in her arms. Her jaw dropped.

'Get away, Mrs Bigibbum!' Richelle screamed, pushing past her and nearly knocking her over. 'Get away! Run!'

The air was filled with the sound of sirens. The police were nearly at the house.

But the man was at the door. He was staggering down the path. We were at the gate by now, but Mrs Vista was still standing and staring in the middle of the path.

'Mrs Vista,' Liz screamed. 'Quickly! Get away from that man!'

She began to go back. I grabbed her arm. 'No, Liz.' I yelled. 'Are you crazy? Leave it to the cops.'

A small white car came around the corner. I looked up eagerly, but it wasn't a police car. It parked neatly by the kerb and Miles Silvestro got out, frowning at us. What's all this? his frown said. Trouble? Just what I thought.

He opened his mouth to say something to us, but before he could speak two police cars rounded the corner and screamed up to the house. Men in uniform jumped to the footpath. Silvestro's eyes popped.

'He's in there,' shouted Sunny, pointing. 'And there's someone else . . .'

'Get back!' a big cop ordered, drawing his gun.

We did what we were told. Quick smart.

On the path Mrs Vista stood motionless, as though she was glued to the spot. By the look on her face she'd finally taken in the situation.

'Goodness, it's poor Mary Vista!' called Silvestro. 'Quick, get her out of there!'

The police moved. But at exactly the same moment the man lunged forward and grabbed Mrs Vista around the waist. She screamed. He reached down to his leg and pulled out a large hunting knife that was strapped to its side. He whipped it up and forced it against Mrs Vista's throat.

'One step closer,' he yelled, 'and she's dead!'

The police froze.

'I mean it!' the man yelled. 'Get out of our way!' He tightened his grip on Mrs Vista's throat. 'Where's your car?' he demanded.

Still clutching the orchid in one arm, Mrs Vista pointed with a shaking finger at a new BMW that was parked just in front of the police cars.

'Give me the keys!' the man demanded.

Mrs Vista still had her car keys in her hand. She lifted them slowly and gave them to him.

'Don't be a fool, mate,' the big cop called. 'You can't get away. Just drop the knife. You'll only make things worse for yourself.'

The man snarled and began moving towards the gate, pushing Mrs Vista in front of him.

The police moved out of the way as he reached the gate.

Mrs Vista's eyes rolled from side to side.

'Drop your guns,' the man said.

'You're crazy, mate,' the big cop said to him. 'You'll never get out of Raven Hill. Roadblocks are going up already.'

'If I die, the old lady dies with me!' the man screamed. 'Drop your guns, and your keys!'

I heard Miles Silvestro whimper.

We watched as the police dropped their guns and threw the keys of the police cars on the grass.

Then the man's eyes slid over to us. They fastened on Sunny, and narrowed.

'All right. Game's over, kid,' he said to her. His hand tightened on the knife. 'Hand over those stones, or the old lady gets it.'

Sunny glanced at me, then looked back at him. 'I haven't got them,' she said calmly.

My mind raced. What was the best thing to do? Was I sure enough of my theory to risk a woman's life?

'Don't give me that,' snarled the man. 'I heard what you said back there in the house.'

I stepped forward. 'She hasn't got the emeralds,' I said. 'I have.'

I heard Liz and Richelle gasp. I felt, rather than saw, the cops leaning towards me, ready for action, Miles Silvestro watching intently.

I dug my hand into my pocket. Pulled out a little plastic bag, glinting green.

The man's eyes fixed on it greedily.

'Here!' I called, and threw it. Then, as he snatched at it, I jumped. Not at him, but at Mrs Vista. I grabbed her around the waist and hauled her away from him, ignoring the knife at her throat. We fell and rolled onto the grass, with dirt from the orchid pot spilling out all over us.

Silvestro yelled. Liz and Richelle screamed. The police sprang forward. And in two minutes the man was flat on the ground, with a couple of big guys on top of him. He was pretty upset. He yelled and swore till his throat must have been red raw.

He could have used those nice green throat soothers I threw to him. But he'd dropped them on the grass. So I picked them up and put them back in my pocket. Waste not, want not.

Mrs Vista staggered to her feet, and clung to me. I put my arm around her waist.

'You save me, Nick,' she burbled.

'He nearly got you killed,' said the big cop.

'It was disgraceful. Disgraceful!' hissed Miles Silvestro. 'Irresponsible! Outrageous!'

Mrs Vista shivered. 'Can I go home now?' she quavered. 'I don't feel so well.'

'Soon,' said the big man gently. 'We'll just take a quick statement.' He patted her arm. Then he turned to me and glared.

'That was a stupid, fool thing to do, you young idiot, playing at being a hero,' he barked. 'This isn't TV you know. He had a knife at her throat. It was a miracle she wasn't killed.'

The others watched me gravely. Then Liz and Sunny moved up to stand beside me. Elmo and Tom crowded in behind. Even Richelle edged a bit closer. They might have thought I'd done the wrong thing. But they weren't going to let me face this alone.

I held Mrs Vista's arm tight. 'Not really,' I said. 'Not such a miracle. I didn't think he'd use the knife.'

'Oh, is that so?' snarled the cop. 'What made you think that?'

I smiled. 'He's a nasty character,' I said. 'But I didn't think he'd kill his mum. Who'd give him his orders then?'

Mrs Vista was stronger than she looked. The push she gave me as she tore herself out of my grip put me on the grass again. She was faster than she looked, too. But she never made it to the car. The cops were faster.

18

Bysie-bye

We watched Mrs Vista and her son being driven away, then went back into the house to wait for the police. Bysie-bye, Mrs Vista, I thought. You thought you'd skip town and leave your son to take the rap, I suppose. Bad luck.

Nobody said much till we got into the living room. Then Tom turned to me.

'Well?' he said.

'Well, what?' I asked.

'Come on, Nick,' Richelle said. 'How did you know Mrs Bigibbum was in on this?'

I pointed at the note still sticking to the glasshouse door.

'Read it,' I said.

'Careful! Don't overwater,' Liz read aloud. 'Leave damp without flooding them. Don't use the orchid food again. Water when plants ready. Remember I'll help. Keep happy, kids, and busy. Then while working you won't get stressed out.'

'So what?' demanded Sunny.

'The reason it sounds weird,' I said, 'is because it's in code.'

'What code?'

'Read every second word.'

'Careful . . . overwater . . . damp,' Elmo read. 'It doesn't make sense.'

'No, skip the first word. Start with "don't". Here, I'll read it: "Don't—leave—without—them. Use—orchid—again—when—ready. I'll—keep—kids—busy—while—you—get—out." See?'

'I get it!' said Elmo. 'She had to send him a coded message. He was in the house, looking for the emeralds. They knew the emeralds were in there somewhere, but they didn't know where. And he couldn't phone his mother because the phone didn't work—thanks to Tom.'

'You're welcome,' Tom said, shining his fingernails on his shirt.

'I never would have suspected Mrs Bigibbum,' Richelle said. 'She was just so—so *embarrassing*. So—*boring*. So—*humble*.'

'Such a good actress,' I said dryly. 'She also knew a lot about her best customer. Little chats every Thursday for a million years must teach you a lot about a person. She'd never been to his house, but she knew bits about it. She knew little bits about all his habits.'

'I guess she did,' sighed Liz. 'She was easy to talk to. She seemed so kind and friendly.'

'And remember, both the rubies last year and the

emeralds this year, were stolen on a *Friday*,' I said. 'Both times Mr T had brought the stones home the day before. Thursday. The same day he bought his weekly flowers.'

'You think Mr Terzis told Mary Vista about the stones?' asked Elmo.

'I'm sure of it,' I said. 'It's just the sort of thing he'd do. "I've got something special in my pocket today, Mary," he'd say, and pat his coat. I can just see him doing it. He'd never suspect she'd be a danger to him. A mumsy, gushing woman like that.'

'There's a lot of guesswork in it, Nick,' Elmo said disapprovingly. I raised my eyebrow at him. What else did he expect?

'Turned out to be right, though, didn't it?' I answered. 'Even the bit about that man being her son. That was a real hunch. The only clue I had was that she said her son had a bad back. That could have been from the car accident. Also I didn't think anyone who wasn't related to her, really under her thumb, would agree to holing up in this house like he did. But it panned out okay.'

'Sure did,' said Liz warmly. 'But Nick, how did he get in here in the first place? We were so careful.'

'Easy,' I said. 'He hid in the bushes next to the front door. When we came out, he slipped in.'

'We would have seen him,' protested Elmo.

'No. Remember when Mrs Vista came with the plant the first time?'

'You mean the time she slipped on the path?' Richelle asked.

'The time she *pretended* to slip. Her son must have been hiding in the bushes then. When we rushed out to help her, he just whipped through the door and ran upstairs.'

'You mean he's been here for two *days?*' exclaimed Tom. '*Living* here? Without anyone knowing?'

'That's right,' I said. 'Looking for the emeralds. They had to do it that way. The house is like a fortress. Once he'd got in, he couldn't get out without his mum's help.'

'I suppose she was going to come and distract us again when the time came,' Liz said. She frowned. I guess she was thinking about how nice she'd been to Mrs Vista when she fell. Liz doesn't like being taken down any more than I do.

'That's right,' I said, grinning at her. 'Of course, when he found the phone wasn't working he had to get a message to his mother somehow. They'd probably organised an emergency system anyway. He used it. He poured something on an orchid—something like turps, maybe—to kill it—'

'There was that funny smell,' nodded Liz.

'Sure. Anyway, he put a message in the dirt under the orchid. And we obligingly took the orchid to his mum. We played postie. And we played it again when we brought her notice back and stuck it on the glasshouse door.'

'They were clever,' said Elmo thoughtfully.

'She was clever,' I said. 'She had me fooled for a while, anyway. But I don't think he was too bright. He was idiotic to show himself to us, for a start. How did he think he was going to get away with it?'

Elmo shuddered. Watching him I remembered how I'd

felt standing in the kitchen just a little time ago, feeling the silence of the house press in on me. Watching the fish cruise in their prison. Feeling trapped. Thinking of blood on the shining, slippery marble floor.

Blood on the floor . . .

'What's the matter, Nick?' Sunny said, tugging at my arm. 'Do you feel sick or something?'

I shook my head slowly. 'No. I was just thinking.'

'Careful, Nick,' said Tom. 'Don't get carried away.'

I smiled at him. 'I was just thinking that that guy really must have been stupid,' I murmured. 'Otherwise he'd have found the emeralds.'

They stared at me.

'What does that say about us, then?' demanded Tom. 'We haven't found them either.'

'I think we have,' I said. 'Follow me.'

We went through the arch to the dining room.

'Tom,' I said. 'You're the tallest.'

I gave him the little bag of green throat soothers. 'Could you hold this in your hand and go to the back door?' I asked.

He made a face, shrugged, and then did as I asked. At the back door he turned back. 'Now what?' he asked, looking around.

'Now run here to us, as fast as you can,' I called.

He did it. He pelted towards us as fast as he could, the plastic bag clutched in his hand. The floor wasn't slippery today, and there were no little dogs barking at his heels, but still the shallow stair between the kitchen and dining areas did its work. Just as I had done, twice, and the masked man had done once, Tom tripped.

I was there to catch him as he fell. But I couldn't catch the plastic bag that flew out of his hand as he clutched desperately at the air to save himself.

It flew up, did a neat arc in the air, and fell down. With a gentle plop. Right into the fish tank.

We crowded around to look. Fish scattered as the packet sank slowly, through the weed, down to the clean, pebbly bottom. We could see it clearly, because although the plastic immediately became invisible in the water, the bright green lollies winked at us, signalling their position.

We strained our eyes. Now everyone knew where to look. And finally, Elmo's breath hissed between his teeth. 'There!' he gasped, pointing. 'There!'

You could barely see it. It was perfectly camouflaged. The stones matched the pebbly fish tank floor. The plastic was transparent in the water. But there it was.

When the police came back into the house, we were fishing with the kitchen tongs. They didn't say anything. They thought all the excitement had made us crazy, I guess.

'How about a statement now, kids?' asked the big cop who'd dealt with Mrs Vista's son.

'One—sec—' I breathed.

'The phone is still out of order, sergeant,' Miles Silvestro shrilled, bustling into the room. 'But I've taken it upon myself to ring Mr Terzis from my car phone. He's coming home. Immediately.'

He turned to us. 'And I have to tell you, Nick, that he's not going to be happy. You children were supposed to be looking after things around here. I know you meant well, but . . .'

Suddenly he noticed what I was doing. 'Nick,' he yelled. 'Stop that! At once! Those fish are worth—'

Got it! I straightened up, smiled at him, put the dripping tongs onto the table and showed him what I held in my hand. He gulped, and goggled at it.

A little plastic bag containing five bits of rock. A million dollars plus. Mr and Mrs Terzis's future. Probably, his job.

The big cop's face stretched into a slow smile.

'Looks like when these kids say they'll look after things, they really mean it,' he said. 'Wouldn't you say, sir?'

Miles Silvestro nodded.

'I suppose so,' he murmured feebly. 'I suppose so.'

Richelle, Elmo, Liz, Tom, Sunny and I looked at each other and grinned.

We have our problems in Teen Power Inc. And I don't suppose the Terzis Castle gig will be the last of them.

But at that moment I have to say that life was very sweet.